Protecting Fiona

Protecting Fiona

SEAL of Protection
Book 3

By Susan Stoker

Table of Contents

Acknowledgements

I think many times people think writing a book is done in isolation, when in reality it's done with the help and support of many people. I just want to acknowledge some of those people here, if you'll indulge me.

Patrick. My husband does a good job of leaving me alone when I'm writing and letting me just…write. Thank you for being my own military man.

Amy. Holy Hell, what would I do without you? You're my cheerleader, my "reader of 1 star reviews", my sounding board, my beta reader, and my friend. Thank you, woman. #youhavenoclue

My Facebook friends. Seriously. All I gotta say is, "I need some help," and I have so many people willing to jump right in and give me suggestions and get my brain working in the right direction. So thank you to all of you for being there for me online.

Michele. Thank you for letting me "steal" your baby's name for my book. The second you told me what you were naming him, I knew I had to use it. Hopefully one day Hunter will see this and know he was "famous" before he was even born!

Dad. I love that you aren't afraid to carry around romance novels with almost-naked men on the cover and hand them out as "tips" to waitresses, hairdressers, and anyone else you come across. Thanks for being one of my biggest fans.

Kathleen Murphy. Thank you for your assistance in my research. I love when friends of friends can connect.

Chris. My graphic designer. Every time someone sees something you've made, they tell me how lucky I am to have a great designer. For someone who has *never* designed anything for a romance author, you've certainly entered a new realm, and knocked it out of the park.

Missy. My editor who makes me feel good by "wanting to throat punch" the mean women in my books even a week after she's read it! And who gives me such great advice. Thank you.

To my readers. Thank you for being interested in my world of hunky, military men. A world where the most important thing in their lives...are their women. If only we lived in a world where every man felt that way. I wish for you all to find your very own "Protector" and to live Happily Ever After.

Special Note from the Author

Protecting Fiona is a made-up story about two women who have been kidnapped and brought to a foreign country with the intent to sell them for sex. While this is a fictional account, this same thing happens all over the world day in and day out. Sex trafficking exists, and there are millions of women and children who have no hope of being rescued.

The International Labor Organization estimates that there are 4.5 million people trapped in forced sexual exploitation globally.

At least 20.9 million adults and children are bought and sold worldwide into commercial sexual servitude, forced labor and bonded labor

Women and girls make up 98% of victims of trafficking for sexual exploitation

An estimated 80% of all trafficked persons are used and abused as sexual slaves.

These statistics are *not* okay.

So while in this story, Julie and Fiona are rescued, there are millions of other women and children out there who are being sexually exploited and will never be rescued. Educate yourself and learn more. You might not feel as if you personally can do anything, but if everyone thought that, how would any of us live in a safe and lawful world?

No matter what country you live in, sexual exploitation and trafficking exists around us. It's a horrifying fact with even more horrifying statistics like I've listed above.

Below are a few websites where you can learn more information. No matter what country you live in, if you do an Internet search, you will find information about trafficking.

http://www.fbi.gov/about-us/investigate/civilrights/human_trafficking
http://www.dhs.gov/blue-campaign
http://ctip.defense.gov/
http://www.equalitynow.org
www.sharedhope.org
http://www.state.gov/j/tip/rls/tiprpt/2014/index.htm
http://www.polarisproject.org/

<u>Warning</u>: Recovering from a sexual assault is not something that happens overnight. It can take years of therapy and help and understanding from family and friends. While this book doesn't describe any kind of sexual assault or rape in detail, reading it might trigger some uncomfortable feelings and thoughts in some readers who have experienced sexual trauma.

Prologue

SIX MEN SAT around a table on the military plane studying a map of the Mexican countryside closely. They were called in for a special assignment. A Senator's daughter had been drugged and kidnapped while she was partying in Las Vegas with friends and hustled over the border before anyone knew she was missing. No ransom note had arrived and that meant the kidnappers were most likely sex traffickers. They wanted a pretty woman they could sell as a sex slave in the bowels of Mexico or beyond.

Wolf, Dude, Abe, Mozart, Benny, and Cookie were all members of the SEAL team that had been chosen to do some recon and see if they couldn't find out where the woman was taken...and bring her home.

The seventh unofficial member of the team, Tex, was in Virginia working his magic with his contacts and computer. In today's day and age, no one was completely off the map. Even terrorists and kidnappers used electronics to communicate with each other. The second they logged onto the Internet, or used a cell phone, Tex would find them.

"Benny, you and Dude will be in charge of extraction. Wait with the helicopter and be ready for the signal," Matthew "Wolf" Steel commanded.

The men nodded in agreement. Benny and Dude had the most experience in flying a helicopter and were the best choices to man the multi-million dollar aircraft. Wolf was the unofficial leader of their group. Every man respected the hell out of him and would follow him into Hell if he asked.

"Abe, you and I will head into the closest village and see what we can find out from the locals. Cookie, you and Mozart will need to check out both of the possible holding sites we've mapped out. This will have to be a 'divide and conquer' mission. We don't have the time to be a hundred percent sure where they're keeping the girl. If you find her, radio back to Benny and Dude, they'll report back to the rest of us and we can all meet up at the coordinates we discussed. Make sure you have the extra set of clothes her father sent, and travel light and fast. We can't afford to fuck this up, and not just because 'Daddy' is a Senator."

Everyone nodded solemnly. They didn't give a rat's ass about what the government or the Senator thought, it was all about the woman. If they didn't find her, and fast, she'd disappear, probably forever, and become just another horrifying statistic.

"Okay, we'll land in about twenty minutes. If I hear anything else from Tex, I'll radio it forward. Let's do this."

Every man nodded in agreement, but not much more was spoken. They were all focused on the upcoming mission.

Hunter "Cookie" Knox cracked his neck and went over in his head his role in the extraction. He was headed toward one of two possible camps where the woman could be. They'd gotten intel that the scumbags who'd usually holed up there were communicating with some known human traffickers. Unfortunately there was *another* group in the same area, one that ran drugs and was known for also selling the occasional woman. This group had also been active recently and the team was looking into them as well.

Mozart would take one group and Cookie would take the other. Cookie hoped like hell he'd find the woman. Orders were to snatch and grab her, but he wouldn't be opposed to taking some of the assholes out. Anyone who thought it was okay to kidnap and sell women deserved to die a slow painful death.

The SEAL team had been on too many rescue missions to count, so unfortunately, this was nothing new, but for some reason Cookie's skin felt too tight. He was way too wound up for this one. He couldn't wait to get boots on the ground and get the woman the hell out of dodge.

The plane started its decent, it was time.

Chapter One

COOKIE WALKED SILENTLY through the jungle, every now and then looking down at the GPS clipped to his LBV, Load Bearing Vest, to make sure he was still heading in the right direction. He could feel the sweat dripping from his forehead and he was constantly wiping it away as he continued ducking and dodging trees and obstacles in his path. Cookie was able to cover a good distance every hour, something he knew he wouldn't be able to do once Julie was with him…if Julie was with him.

Even though their intel told them that it was likely she was being held in one of the two camps, Cookie hoped like hell their information was correct. Sex trafficking wasn't anything that followed patterns. One time a group might keep a woman for weeks, another woman might be held for only hours. It depended on where, and who, she was headed for.

Even though Cookie was paying attention where he was placing his feet, he still found himself stumbling over roots and mud on the ground. The jungle wasn't anyplace anyone would ever take a pleasure hike, and Cookie knew the walk back to the extraction point with Julie wasn't going to be easy. Hell, it wasn't easy for him, and he was trained, and dressed, for it.

The Senator had given them clothes for his daughter, but even a long sleeve shirt and a pair of pants couldn't keep the mosquitos out of their eyes and the heat from permeating the very morrow of their bones as they walked back to the extraction point. Cookie knew he'd never take air conditioning for granted again.

He slowed his pace as he got close to his target. The camp was noisy and bustling. The men were consuming large quantities of alcohol and it was obvious they were celebrating something. Cookie kneeled down in the darkness the jungle provided and bided his time. He wanted to rush to the most likely building, sitting off to the side, but he made himself wait. He only had one chance to do this right, and Julie was counting on him to get her out of there. Cookie would wait until the right time. Then he'd make his move.

FIONA SAT IN the dark, eyes straining. She wasn't sleeping well, as usual, and had listened while her captors had partied the night away. They'd grown quiet an hour or so ago and she knew morning was on its way.

Fiona had been thinking about how quiet it was, now that the men were most likely passed out, when she thought she heard something. She wasn't sure if it was her imagination or the drugs they'd been forcing on her, but she didn't think it was either. Fiona knew every creak and moan in her hellhole, and the sound she heard was out of the ordinary.

Julie, the other woman, was finally silent. She'd cried nonstop for two days. It wasn't as if Fiona was cold hearted, but Julie wouldn't listen to her and wouldn't be consoled. Fiona tried to remember back to when she was first brought here, but it was impossible. It was just too long ago. She thought it had been around three months, but she couldn't be sure. Fiona had tried to keep track, but she knew there were some days that she'd been out of it from the drugs her captors been forcing on her. Ninety days, one hundred days…whatever it was, it was a lifetime.

There. A small beam of light in the corner. Fiona knew it wasn't the guards, they weren't going to sneak around, and they certainly wouldn't just have a small flashlight. Who was it? What was it? Fiona was afraid to hope.

Fiona knew no one was coming for her. She didn't have any family back home, and her friends were more acquaintances than anything else. She knew how these things worked. When someone was kidnapped, the family would do whatever it took it get back their loved one…but in her case, she had no one. Fiona was at the mercy of the kidnappers, had been at their mercy for three long months, and no one was going to rescue her.

Her mind almost veered toward the hell she'd been through at the kidnappers' hands, but Fiona clamped it down. She couldn't go there. Didn't know if she'd ever be able to go there again. Her new mantra was to survive one day at a time, but even that little rebellion against her captors was on shaky ground. Fiona had slowly picked up some Spanish during her captivity, and the words she'd been able to translate, namely, drug, die, bitch, and dirt, weren't making her think happy thoughts. But Fiona would much rather face death head-on then suffer through whatever the men had in store for Julie. No contest.

COOKIE HAD BEEN dropped off five miles away by Dude and Benny in the chopper. The plan was to grab the woman, and set off back through the jungle. Cookie was prepared for anything, or so he thought. He half chuckled to himself. Hell, they *tried* to be prepared for anything, but as they usually found out Plan A usually didn't work, and Plan B typically became the new Plan A. Every now and then the team would have to come up with a Plan C on the fly when both the other plans became FUBAR, fucked up beyond all recognition.

Cookie stealthily made his way toward the ramshackle building at the edge of the camp. It was early in the morning, and pitch dark. He'd watched as the men in the camp drunk themselves into a stupor and staggered around the camp. Some fell in the dirt and their so-called buddies just left them there to sleep off the alcohol.

They'd been partying for a reason; these types of men didn't have money to waste on getting drunk every night. Cookie hoped like hell he was in the right place. They could be celebrating selling the woman he was here to find. He hoped he wasn't too late. If they'd already sold Julie, there was little chance the team would be able to get her back. She'd disappear, just as hundreds of women did every year.

Cookie turned his penlight on for just a moment so he could get his bearings. There was no noise coming from the small rectangular building. His intelligence said the woman could be here, and the men's actions outside seemed to confirm it. Mozart was about twenty clicks north of his location, checking out a second possible site. The twelve miles or so between them might as well have been a hundred. Mozart was too far away to provide backup, and the reverse was true as well.

If the building was empty, Cookie would fade away back into the jungle and meet back up with Wolf and

Abe who were waiting in the closest town for the results of their investigations.

The woman that he'd come after, Julie, had been missing for five days. Five days of Hell. Five days too long in Cookie's opinion. Hell, *one* day was too long.

Cookie and his SEAL team brothers had seen all of this before. He'd never get used to the fact that humans were sold for sex slaves. It was so barbaric. Cookie thought about his teammates' women being in this type of situation and it made his skin crawl. Caroline and Alabama were two of the strongest women he knew. Caroline had saved Wolf's life twice. Cookie knew women were stronger, in general, than most men gave them credit for.

But this, being kidnapped and knowing you were to be sold into a life of abuse and sexual depravity never to be free again, that was something Cookie didn't know how anyone could survive with their sanity intact.

Julie was the daughter of a Senator, and probably one of the only reasons Cookie and his team were in Mexico. If it had been anyone else, any other less-rich, less-politically motivated father, the family would've had to try to work with the local police, or private investigators, and gotten nowhere. Cookie went back to his thought that no woman, no *human*, should have to go through what Julie what had inevitably gone through since she'd been kidnapped. Cookie figured she'd probably been raped repeatedly to try to scare her into submission. She was probably starved and scared out of her mind. Cookie knew Julie would most likely need years of counseling to help her become normal again...*if* he could find her and get her out of the jungle safely.

If Julie could walk, it'd make his job easier, but he was prepared to carry her if he needed to. Cookie knew she was a small woman, only about five feet two inches tall and weighing about a hundred and ten pounds. He figured she'd probably lost weight the week she'd been in captivity, so he knew he wouldn't have any issues carrying her through the jungle if he needed to.

The pack he normally carried on missions weighed about what Julie did, but Cookie had gone light for this trip. He carried only the bare necessities for their trek back through the thick trees. He wanted to be able to move quickly and silently, and that'd be easier if he had less weight to carry.

Cookie also had his first aid kit so he could help Julie in any medical way if she needed it, and she probably would. Human traffickers weren't known to be the nicest of people. The change of clothes he'd brought in her size would protect her from the insects and plants as they cut back through the jungle to the extraction point. He was carrying extra water and food rations for the two of them for a day or two as well.

Cookie moved silently to the building and shone his

light briefly on the corner. Bingo. The boards were rotted here from the heat and wetness of the jungle. They'd be easier to remove. Cookie knew the kidnappers were in the other buildings, most of them passed out, but he wasn't taking any chances. He wanted to get Julie and get the hell out of there without anyone noticing. If luck was with him, he and Julie would be long gone before the kidnappers realized she'd escaped.

Cookie removed two boards, just enough for him to squeeze through, and eased himself into the room, not knowing what he'd find. He didn't want to just shine his light into the room because if it wasn't where Julie was being held, he could be in a rash of shit.

Fiona held her breath. She could hear whoever it was working on the wall in the corner. She'd thought many times that if she could only reach the walls she could escape out into the jungle…but since she was chained to the floor, she couldn't get anywhere near them. She watched as a man, Fiona assumed it was a man, eased himself into the room.

There was only the light coming in from the moonlight through the hole he'd made in the wall, but since Fiona's eyes were adjusted to the darkness, she could see surprisingly well. The man was big, and had a large pack on his back. He wore all black and was focused on Julie, who was lying on the floor on his side of the room. Since she was on the other side of the rectangular building, Fiona didn't think the man could see her through the inky blackness of the night.

Cookie tried to breathe through his nose. The smell in the room was putrid. It smelled like urine, sweat, blood, and fear. Some people would scoff at his saying he could smell fear, but Cookie had been in enough hell holes, and seen enough bad shit in his career, to know that fear had an odor. It wasn't something he could readily explain to someone else, but anyone who'd been in combat and had seen the things he had, would know immediately what he meant.

He'd been in a lot of bad places with his SEAL team, but this was one of the worst. Cookie hadn't thought the sex traffickers had the woman long enough for it to get this bad, but he supposed anything was possible. Everyone dealt with the shit that happened in their lives differently, and because Julie was from a rich, powerful family, Cookie supposed she didn't have the coping mechanisms other people did.

Cookie saw a shape on the floor that had to be Julie. His pulse shot up even higher than it already was. The adrenaline coursed through his body. He'd found her. Thank God.

"Julie," Cookie whispered, while briefly touching her shoulder.

The woman rolled over, looked up and took a huge intake of breath. Knowing what was coming, Cookie quickly put his hand over Julie's mouth to stifle her scream. He quickly tried to reassure her.

"My name is Cookie, I'm an American Navy SEAL. I'm here to take you home." His words were toneless and quiet. They barely penetrated the few inches from his mouth to her ears, but she heard them nonetheless.

Julie nodded frantically and started to cry. "Thank God," she whispered brokenly after Cookie had removed his hand from her mouth.

Cookie didn't waste any time trying to reassure her further, but instead got to work freeing her. He was pissed. Julie was attached to the floor by a short chain attached around her ankle. She had some freedom of movement, but not a lot. There was a bucket nearby, Cookie assumed for Julie to relieve herself in.

"Can you stand? Can you walk?" Cookie asked Julie, again in the toneless quiet voice he'd used before.

Julie nodded, but swayed when she stood up. Cookie dug in his pack and got out the black long sleeved shirt he'd brought for her. She was small, almost dainty, and fragile looking. Cookie helped Julie put each arm through the sleeves. He then took out the black cargo pants. Eying Julie's build, he thought they might actually be a bit big, but he hoped they'd do.

"Julie, take off your shorts and put these on, quickly." Cookie wasn't known as being a gentle man, and he couldn't help it if he sounded short. He knew time was against them, they had to get out of there and disappear into the jungle before the kidnappers started sobering up and came to haul Julie out of there and give her to her new owner.

"What?" Julie said huffily, "I couldn't possibly with you here…"

Cookie cut her off with a hand over her mouth again. "Look, do you want to get out of here or not? You can't walk out in that jungle with shorts on, just put the damn pants on."

Cookie half turned to give Julie as much privacy as he could. He didn't like the whiny tone of her voice, but tried to give her the benefit of the doubt. She was scared out of her mind. He could try harder to be pleasant. Cookie tried to imagine Caroline or Alabama in Julie's shoes. The thought made him soften his voice. "I'm sorry, I didn't mean to be so abrupt. Let me know when you're ready."

"Please, let's just go," was Julie's response. Cookie turned and saw that she'd put the pants on and was holding onto the waist with one hand. The pants fit, but barely. Cookie steadied her when she stumbled as she lurched toward the corner of the room where he'd entered. Julie's hand gripped his shirt into a ball as they headed for the exit.

As Cookie turned to leave the room, he took one last glance around the long room and stilled and narrowed his eyes. He thought he saw something at the other side. Was he seeing things? Cookie cocked his head and strained to listen. Were they about to be caught? Was it one of the men? Cookie gripped the knife at his waist and waited, every muscle ready to leap into action.

Chapter Two

FIONA WATCHED DISPASSIONATELY as the man who'd snuck into their prison helped Julie into a long-sleeved shirt. Fiona didn't move a muscle. It was obvious that the man had come for the slight woman and not for her. Even though Fiona hoped and prayed someone would find her, it hurt that he'd come for Julie and not her. She was a big girl; she'd survived everything they'd done to her so far, she'd survive this too.

All Fiona could do was look on helplessly. She wouldn't cry, she wouldn't beg. She thought about calling out to the man, but he was obviously trying to be quiet and last thing she wanted to do was alert the kidnappers of what was going on, that their latest slave was being rescued.

Fiona watched as the man turned away to give Julie some privacy to put on the pants he'd brought her. She couldn't hear what he'd said to her, his voice was pitched too low for it to carry across the room. Fiona hadn't known many men that were honorable, but it seemed that this soldier was one; at least he understood Julie might be embarrassed or traumatized about taking off her shorts in front of him after everything she'd been through.

She watched as the pair turned to leave through the now-missing boards in the corner. Fiona held her breath. She tried to tell herself it was a miracle that at least one of them would get out of this hellhole. Maybe Julie would tell someone about her once she was away from there and safe.

Just as the pair was about to leave, the man turned to take one last look around the room. Fiona watched as he went perfectly still, while seemingly looking right at her. She knew she hadn't made any noise. Had she? Had she unconsciously moved or done something to gain his attention? Had he seen her? How had he known she was there?

Cookie put his hand on Julie's arm and whispered, "Wait right here. I thought I saw something."

"Where are you going?" Julie screeched quietly and grabbed his arm desperately. "No, don't go over there….we have to go; please I want to go right now!"

Cookie put up his hand to silence her and pried her hand off his arm. "Quiet. Do you want everyone in camp coming in here to see why you're making so much noise?" At Julie's quick head shake, he continued. "Right. Now stay here for a second, I'll be right back."

Cookie slipped into the darkness toward the other side of the room. He thought he'd seen someone else in the room, his knife at the ready. If it was one of the bad guys, he'd have to take him out. He couldn't leave any witnesses as to what happened to Julie. As soon as he'd had the thought he dismissed it. It couldn't have been one of the kidnappers, he would've been confronted by now. Cookie was confused, if it was another prisoner why hadn't the person said anything? Was he seeing things? If it was another person, why hadn't Tex said anything about a second prisoner? Tex had been illegally monitoring the area with the highly sensitive government satellites, he should've known about a second person in the building with Julie.

Cookie and his team were always prepared for anything, but if it *was* another person, or God forbid, more than one person, this rescue just got one hundred percent more complicated. They hadn't counted on more than Julie, not even Plan B had accounted for more than one prisoner. Cookie tried to mentally calculate the provisions he had with him, along with the extraction procedures as he crept on silent feet to the other side of the long empty space. Everything would have to be altered depending on what he found.

Cookie moved silently along the wall toward where he thought he'd seen something. As he moved, the stench in the room got stronger. If there was someone else here, they'd been here a lot longer than Julie had been, based on the smell alone. He tried not to gag, to react, as he moved closer. Cookie stopped suddenly. Holy shit. It *was* another person, another prisoner. It was a woman.

She looked horrible. She was also chained to the floor, but she'd been chained by the neck instead of by the ankle, as Julie had been. She was sitting with her legs to the side on the floor, with one hand propping her up. She was covered in dirt and filth. He could see the whites of her eyes shining through the grime on her face. The light was almost nonexistent back here, but Cookie could see all too clearly the shape she was in.

She was wearing a raggedy T-shirt, cut off jean shorts that had seen better days, and there was a pair of flip flops sitting next to her on the floor. She sat there staring at him silently.

Fiona watched the man approach her. As she guessed, he was some sort of soldier. She suddenly had the horrible thought that maybe he wasn't here to rescue Julie, but instead to steal her from their captors to sell her himself. Fiona took a deep breath. No, she had to believe he was there to save Julie, not put her through more hell.

Fiona saw the man take her in in a single glance. She could only guess what she looked like. She knew she was filthy and smelled horrid. Her captors hadn't allowed her to shower and the only way to see to her needs was the bucket nearby, which hadn't been emptied in way too long.

They'd tortured her by shortening her chain and attaching it to her neck rather than her ankle so she didn't have much freedom of movement. Fiona only had enough room to stand up if she hunched over, and only enough to move two feet from one side to another. She was still wearing the same clothes they'd taken her in. She was disgusting, Fiona knew it. She hadn't worried about it before, rightfully thinking it helped keep her abuse to a minimum, but now...now she cared.

Fiona wasn't sure what to say to the man. She was embarrassed and desperately wanted to get out of there, but she knew that no one had paid for him to get *her* out, only the other woman. Maybe she could convince him to tell the government or the Army, or *someone*, that she was there so they could come back and get her. Fiona knew there was no way this man could take her with him too. It was okay; she tried to tell herself, really.

Cookie couldn't help but be shocked. And he wasn't easily shocked. The types of missions he and his team had been on had, for the most part, all been awful. While some had good outcomes, none were anything he ever wanted to re-live. This trumped them all.

The woman sat on the floor, surrounded by filth,

chained to the floor, and just looked at him. Cookie couldn't believe she hadn't said anything the whole time he was there. He almost left without knowing she was there.

"Do you speak English? What's your name?" Cookie asked softly as he kneeled down next to her and reached for his knife.

"Fiona," she said softly, with no discernible accent.

American, Cookie thought to himself, *probably from the Midwest.*

"We've got to hurry, Fiona," he said to her distractedly. He said it as much to her as he did to himself. Cookie wasn't thinking much about her at the moment, his mind was preoccupied with coming up with a new plan on how to get both her and Julie out of the jungle unscathed. He had no clothes for this woman. They'd only planned on Julie. Cookie thought about what he had in his pack. He could give her the extra shirt he'd brought for himself, but he couldn't do anything about her shoes or her shorts. *Shit, this was going to be tough.*

In the midst of thinking through a new escape plan, Cookie also thought back to Julie's actions. She was going to let them walk out of the room without once saying anything about another person being held with her. Julie was going to let this woman, Fiona, die, or at least be put through more hell. Cookie had met some selfish people in his life, but he'd never thought that anyone could be as callous as Julie had just been. Cookie tried to concentrate back on Fiona and not think about Julie for a moment.

Fiona put out her hand to touch the man, then changed her mind and put it back in her lap. She was amazed the soldier was going to try to break her chain, but he really didn't have the time. They had to get out of there before they were discovered.

"It's okay, Sir," Fiona said as softly as she could. "I know you're here for her," she gestured toward Julie who was a dark blob on the other side of the room, impatiently waiting by the corner, "and don't have time for me, but if you could maybe tell the Army, or police, or *someone*, that I'm here when you get home, I'd appreciate it."

Cookie stilled and looked at the woman. Had he heard her right? "Pardon?" he asked before he could stop himself.

Fiona almost cried. He sounded mad. She didn't want to make him mad. She stuttered a bit in responding, and dropped her voice a bit more. Fiona was embarrassed for Julie to hear how pathetic she really was. "I-I-I don't have any money to hire you to get me away too, so if you could just tell someone when you leave…" she trailed off as the man continued to stare at her.

Finally he said in a clipped tone, "If you think I'm

leaving you here, you're crazy."

As Fiona opened her mouth, he quietly shushed her and got to work on the chain around her neck.

Cookie was pissed. What the hell? Why would this woman think he'd leave her here? As much as having her along was going to be an inconvenience, it wasn't impossible. Nothing was impossible, every SEAL had that pounded into them from day one of their training. Cookie couldn't carry both this woman and Julie, so he hoped one of them would be able to walk on their own. Fiona was painfully thin, but tall. As Cookie leaned toward her, he tried to breathe through his mouth. The stench was horrific, but he knew it would embarrass her if he made any mention of it, consciously or unconsciously.

"I'm sorry that I stink," Fiona told him softly, as if she could read his mind.

Cookie quietly shushed her again. He didn't know how else to respond. He couldn't deny that she stank, but he also didn't want to say that it didn't bother him. Cookie didn't have time to get into all the things he wanted to say to her and to ask her.

He concentrated harder on the chain. He knew time wasn't on their side. Finally Cookie said to her, "I can't get the metal collar off right now, but I can break the chain."

Fiona simply said, "Okay," as if the heavy metal collar around her neck was a beautiful gold delicate necklace instead of a torture device that had to be causing her pain.

When the chain finally fell free, Cookie eased it to the ground so it wouldn't clank loudly. He quickly turned back to his pack and dug deep until he came up with his extra shirt. It was long sleeved and black, just like the one he had on. He held it out to Fiona.

"I don't have any extra pants, but I do have a shirt, it'll be big on you but it'll help some. It's better than nothing."

Fiona nodded, inordinately pleased to have even that. "Thank you. Seriously, I…it'll be perfect."

Cookie continued speaking. "I don't have any shoes that will fit you or an extra pair of pants," he told her, voicing his worries out loud.

Fiona knew that walking through the jungle in shorts and flip flops was going to suck, which was probably the understatement of the century, but she certainly wasn't going to complain. The collar around her neck hurt. It had rubbed her skin raw and she thought she was bleeding, but again, Fiona would volunteer to wear the thing forever if it meant getting out of this hellhole.

"I can manage with just the shirt, thank you," Fiona told him honestly. At his look of disbelief that she misinterpreted, she straightened a bit and vowed, "I won't slow you down. I know you don't have to help me, but I swear I'll be quiet and I'll keep up. I'll do whatever you tell me to, I'll do anything to get out of here."

Cookie looked at Fiona in surprise. She kept impressing the hell out of him. She could've been hysterical, but she had a quiet dignity about her. He wished he could take the time to get to know more about what the hell had happened to her and how she'd gotten there, but he was quickly running out of time.

"That's good to hear, Fiona. Just talk to me as we go," Cookie told her. "I'll do what I can to help you, but if you don't tell me something is wrong or that you need assistance, I can't help you."

Fiona nodded and told him, "If I *do* slow you down too much, just go on without me. I'll either catch up or you can send someone back for me later."

Cookie just shook his head. "Not gonna happen, Fiona," he told her. "We're all getting out of here together."

Cookie stood and reached down to help Fiona up. He grasped her by the upper arm. He shouldn't have been surprised at how fragile she felt, but he was. Her quiet strength as she'd spoken had distracted him to her true physical state.

He felt her sway a bit, but she caught herself and straightened quickly. Cookie heard her take one quick inhale of breath and then quiet herself. He watched as Fiona hobbled awkwardly over to her flip-flops and slipped them onto her feet. She nodded awkwardly, because of the metal collar, as if to tell him she was ready to go.

Cookie grabbed her hand and squeezed, something he didn't have to do, and normally didn't do, but he wanted to show this woman that everything would be all right. There was just something about her that made him want to reassure her. The team had been taught when rescuing civilians from uncertain situations, not to touch them unnecessarily. They had no idea what they'd been through and what might be a trigger for them. The last thing the team needed was someone flipping out or reacting badly in the middle of a volatile situation.

Cookie had no idea if everything would work out all right, they were far from safe, she was far from being rescued, but he needed Fiona to know he was impressed with her. He wanted to convey so much with that one small hand squeeze. Cookie didn't know her story, but he would soon. He just had to get them all out of here in one piece.

Fiona fought back her tears. Jesus, she had to get it together. His small sign of approval and encouragement was all it took for her to want to fall into his arms and never let go. She couldn't do anything to distract or irritate this man. He was all that was standing between her and freedom.

She trudged behind him as quietly as she could as they crossed back to the hole in the corner of the room. Fiona flinched as her shoes made a *thunking* noise every time she took a step. Flip-flops weren't exactly quiet. She began to shuffle her feet instead, and the noise quieted.

Fiona watched as the soldier lay on his stomach and scooted out the hole first. He'd told both her and Julie to wait until he'd checked out the immediate area to make sure it was safe. Fiona took the moment to sit on the floor and rest. Jesus, even the short walk across the room tired her out. She had no idea how she was going to make it out in the jungle, but she'd do her best as long as she could.

As if reading her mind, Julie leaned over and grabbed Fiona's arm with a surprisingly strong grip and dug her nails in. "You better not screw this up for me. My daddy sent him for *me*, not for your sorry ass."

Fiona jerked her arm out of Julie's grip and scooted away from the other woman. She didn't say anything. She couldn't. Every vile word out of Julie's mouth was the truth and couldn't be refuted.

Cookie found the camp much the way it was when he'd entered the building the women had been held in. No one was up and about; they were all still sleeping or passed out. They didn't have much time before the sun started rising and they had to be long gone by then. Cookie headed back to the building and helped Julie slither out of the hole. He motioned for her to crouch by the wall, then he turned to help Fiona.

After both women were out, Cookie propped the boards back up in their original places. It wouldn't pass a close inspection, but hopefully the kidnappers weren't that smart and wouldn't have any idea how their prisoners escaped for a long while, giving them a nice head start.

"Come on, ladies, let's get out of here."

Cookie watched as both women nodded enthusiastically, and they all headed off into the unforgiving jungle.

Chapter Three

FIONA TRUDGED ALONG behind the soldier and Julie silently. She'd vowed not to do anything to hold them up, and she was doing her damnedest to keep that vow. It was still dark out, but the sun had just started to make its way above the horizon. Fiona could barely see Julie ahead of her. The other woman was holding on to the backpack of the soldier for dear life. Julie hadn't let Fiona get anywhere near the man, she'd claimed him for herself.

He was setting a good pace and Fiona could hear herself breathing too hard and too loud. She'd stopped swatting at the bugs on her legs a while back, it was useless and pointless. As soon as she swatted one away, two more would land. Fiona knew she'd have bug bites all over, but she'd be alive. Her feet also hurt. She'd stubbed her toes more than once on the logs and other things on the forest floor, but she wasn't going to complain. Fiona refused to bitch about it. She was out of that hellhole and she'd endure whatever she had to in order to get out of the country altogether.

Fiona *was* worried about the drug withdrawal she knew she was going into. Her body had started to shake and she knew it was only a matter of time before the craving for the drugs her captors forced into her system would get bad. She had no idea what the hell they were shooting into her body, but hated every second of it. The feeling of some mysterious cocktail being shoved into her veins was awful. She'd fought her captors like a wildcat every time they came in with another syringe. They'd just hold her down as they shoved the needle into her arm. Fiona had gone through withdrawal several times since they'd begun shooting her up, and her captors had just laughed at her. They'd watched her, waiting for her to beg for the drugs, but Fiona refused. No way in hell was she gonna beg the assholes to put more poison in her body. Finally they'd gotten bored of their little game, and injected the drug into her body regularly, not caring that she fought them every time.

Fiona had to take her mind off of the drugs and her body's reaction…she did what she had done while chained to the floor…she started concentrating on counting backward from one thousand slowly. If she concentrated on the numbers everything else seemed to be better. *One thousand, nine hundred ninety nine, nine hundred ninety eight.*

When Fiona had counted down to the three hundreds, the soldier came to a stop. The morning light was peeking through the trees now, heating the area up quickly.

"We'll stop here for a break," he told the women.

Julie immediately sat down. "Please," she said in a whiny voice. "I'm so hungry, do you have any food?"

Cookie looked at the woman sitting at his feet. Of course she was hungry, but he'd wanted to get them as far away from the compound before stopping. He remembered back to the hellhole he'd found Julie in and thought about how she'd wanted to leave Fiona behind. He tried to hold back his annoyance. Julie *had* been kidnapped for Christ's sake.

"Of course, Julie. I've got some granola bars."

Julie snapped, "That's it? Only granola bars? Do you know how long it's been since I've had any kind of *real* food?"

Cookie paused in the act of reaching into his pack and simply stared at the woman. He was getting pissed. Was she serious? Of course she was. He tried to stay civil.

"Yes, that's it. You'll be away from here soon enough and will be able to have a full meal then. It's not a good idea to eat a big meal right now when your stomach isn't used to it. You'll want to start out slowly and get used to regular sized meals again. I've also got some water. You both," he continued, including Fiona in his gesture, "will need to be sure to drink some."

Fiona's mouth watered uncontrollably. She stood off to the side of Julie and the man, leaning against a tree. She hadn't wanted to sit down, knowing she might not be able to get up again. Besides, as sore as she was, it felt great to stand fully upright, something she hadn't been able to do for a while. The chain around her neck had prevented it. Her back hurt from the walk and unaccustomed exercise, but it felt so good to be in the fresh air and upright, she wasn't about to complain about it.

And granola bars. God. It'd been so long since Fiona had eaten real food, just as Julie had said. Of course *her* "long time" was quite a bit longer than Julie's had been. Sometimes her captors would bring her some potato chips or something, but usually they'd just throw in a piece of hard bread. Fiona wasn't sure how long it had been since she'd had something that wasn't moldy or stale.

And fresh water? She was in heaven. It was amazing how the little things meant so much more when you didn't have them. She'd been drinking crappy water for longer than she remembered. At first she was sick as a dog from drinking whatever her captors brought to her, but eventually her body got used to the bacteria and whatever other organisms were swimming in the water. Her stomach still hurt sometimes from the parasites Fiona knew were probably coursing through her body, but at least she wasn't constantly sick anymore. Fiona wanted to jump the man, grab the food, and stuff it in her mouth as fast as she could. But she couldn't. She didn't know how much food he had brought, and she was extra baggage. Fiona figured she'd waited this long, she could wait a bit longer to get something to eat if there wasn't enough…maybe.

Cookie walked over to where Fiona was leaning against a tree. If he thought she looked bad before, in the light of the new day he could see she looked worse than he'd thought. He hadn't been able to see her very well in the building, and they'd been walking in the dark since then, but now that Cookie had the chance to really look at her, he wasn't sure how she was still standing.

The metal collar was partially hidden by his black T-shirt, but he could see Fiona's skin around the top of it was red and painful looking. Cookie couldn't see any blood, but it wouldn't surprise him if she was bleeding where the collar dug into her neck. Her legs were filthy, and he could see they were covered in welts from bug bites. Her feet in the flip-flops were absolutely disgusting, covered in mud and caked with black stuff up to her knees. She'd pulled back her hair at some point and secured it with a vine from one of the trees they'd passed. It was stringy and limp and badly in need of some soap. Her face and hands were also covered in dirt and she had rivulets of sweat running down her temples.

She was also very skinny, too skinny. She'd obviously not had enough to eat in far too long. Cookie held out a wet-wipe that he'd pulled from his bag and offered it to Fiona without a word.

Fiona looked at the man and at the wet wipe he held out. She wanted to snatch it up and revel in the cleanness of it, but she hesitated.

Cookie saw her hesitation and said softly, misunderstanding her reticence. "I know it's not much, but until we can get further away, we can't risk a full bath." Fiona nodded. It was silly, but she didn't want to be partially clean. It'd just bring home to her how awful the rest of her felt and smelled if she cleaned just a part of her.

As if he could read her mind, the gorgeous man in front of her said, "At least your hands, Fiona. Then you can eat without worrying about germs."

Fiona laughed without humor. "I don't think I have to worry about germs. I don't want to take your last one," she told him being honest.

"I have plenty," Cookie told her, still holding out the cloth.

Fiona finally reached out for the wet wipe slowly, embarrassed at how badly her hands were shaking. She tried to smile at the man, hoping he wouldn't notice. Of course he did.

"Are you okay?" Cookie said softly, narrowing his

eyes, "Your hands are shaking."

Fiona concentrated on rubbing her hands and wouldn't look him in the eye as she tried to scrub three months of crud from her hands. "I'm good. I'm just really ready to get out of here."

Cookie watched the woman in front of him. Holy Hell. Where did she get her strength from? He knew of a lot of men that could endure great pain and had awesome endurance. He'd seen it time and time again with his own teammates. But standing there, watching this woman nonchalantly try clean her hands and ignore her hunger and the fact she'd just escaped after being held captive for who knew how long... Cookie thought she had to be one of the most mentally strong women he'd ever met, and that included Wolf's woman, Caroline.

Cookie almost forgot he'd brought her a granola bar, but finally remembered. "When you're done, be sure to give me back the wipe. We don't want to leave any sign we've been here." He watched Fiona nod, still not looking at him. "Then you can eat your granola bar and we can be on our way."

Cookie watched as she did finally look up at that, not at him, but at the food he held out toward her. Fiona's eyes were locked on the food in his hand as if she blinked, it would disappear. He could almost see her salivating. The muscle in her jaw ticked as she ground her teeth together and Cookie could see her swallow several times. She might outwardly act like it didn't matter if she ate anything or not, but he could see in her eyes how desperate she was for the little piece of food he held out to her. Her breathing had increased and he could almost see her heart beating in her chest. She swallowed twice more, struggling with herself.

Fiona wanted that granola bar more than she'd ever wanted anything before, well maybe not more than getting out of this jungle. She dropped her eyes and shrugged, trying to look disinterested. She looked back down at her hands, now absently rubbing them, and told him, "It's okay, I'm not hungry, you can save it for later."

Cookie barely kept his mouth from dropping open. The woman was skin and bones, he knew she was hungry, starving in fact, and she was refusing the food? What the hell?

"Fiona, you need the strength to continue. You need to eat."

Just as Fiona opened her mouth to respond, Julie interrupted. "I'll eat it if she doesn't want it."

Fiona swallowed hard and tried not to cry. Her stomach rebelled at the thought of giving the granola bar away, but she controlled herself and forced herself to whisper to Cookie, "Julie can have it. I'll just have some water."

Uh, no. Cookie took Fiona by the arm and led her a bit away, saying sternly over his shoulder to Julie, "We'll be right back, stay put."

"What is *up* with you?" Cookie asked Fiona with little patience in his voice. He didn't have time for this. This was why he didn't have a steady girlfriend. He'd never understand the games women played if he lived to be a hundred. "I have to get you both to the extraction point. I need you to walk, I can't carry you *and* her at the same time," Cookie scolded bluntly. "I can only carry one of you at a time."

"You won't need to carry me. I told you I won't slow you down. I know I'm extra baggage you didn't expect. I won't get in your way, I won't slow you down and I won't eat the food so that there isn't enough. You only planned for two, you didn't plan for me."

Cookie calmed down. So that was it. She wasn't trying to play him in any way, she wasn't playing games, she was trying to fly under his radar. He didn't want to burst her bubble, but it wasn't working.

"Look," Cookie tried to reassure Fiona, putting a hand on her shoulder briefly, "it's not that far to the extraction point. I have plenty of food for us all, even though I didn't expect you. Eating one granola bar will not deplete my resources. I was going to wait to tell you both this at the same time, but I obviously need to let you know now. I'm part of a Navy SEAL team that was dropped here to get Julie out. My teammates are nearby. We'll meet at the extraction point and get the hell out of here. No more talk about being 'extra' okay? Now, please, you need the energy and the calories, Fiona. Take it."

Fiona didn't look like she believed him, either about the help coming or about the amount of food he had for them, but she was literally starving. Cookie almost chuckled at the obvious indecision on her face, but he saw the moment she made her decision.

Fiona couldn't make herself reach out for the granola bar when he again held out it out to her, but she knew she needed it so she'd be able to continue. She looked up at the man, not knowing how her eyes pleaded with him to take the decision out of her hands.

Cookie reached out and gently took one of her shaking hands and held on when Fiona would've jerked it back. He waited until she looked up at him. "I swear to you, Fiona, you are *not* extra baggage. Yes, we were sent here for Julie, but I would've come by myself if I had known you were there. I would have come for *you*."

Fiona just stared at him, willing her tears away. After not hearing a kind word in so long, his words felt like balm to her blistered soul. He'd never know how much what he'd just said meant to her.

Cookie wanted to say more. He wanted to say that he admired her, that he was amazed by her, but he knew it wasn't the time or the place. He dropped his hand and Fiona was left holding the granola bar. Cookie watched as she tried to open the snack. She fumbled with the thick plastic and couldn't grip it hard enough to rip it open. Cookie took it and tore it open for her, then handing it back to her without the wrapper.

Fiona took a small bite and closed her eyes. It was the best thing she'd ever eaten, *ever*. She tried to savor the flavors and not chew too fast. She finally finished the first bite, swallowed, and opened her eyes again to take another small bite and met the man's eyes. Fiona turned away in embarrassment. God, she was such a dork. She should just eat the stupid thing and be done with it, but it'd been so long, she wanted to savor the granola as long as she could.

Cookie swallowed his anger. He was furious. Not at Fiona, but at the creeps who'd held her for so long. The pleasure on her face from that one small bite hit him hard. He'd never been so hungry that one bite of food was total bliss. Of course during SEAL training and BUD/S, he and his buddies had *thought* they were going to die of hunger, but from the look on Fiona's face just now, he knew they hadn't even been close.

He turned away to give Fiona some privacy and went back over to where he'd left Julie resting. Cookie knew he sounded harsher than he wanted when he told the women a little while later that it was time to continue on. Julie groaned and whined about how much she hurt, but she got up, grabbed onto his pack, and they were ready to go again.

Chapter Four

FIONA KEPT QUIET as they walked. She concentrated on making the granola bar last as long as she could. She took tiny bites and counted every chew she made. It not only made the food last longer, but it took her mind off of how horrible she felt.

Her stomach hurt, but Fiona knew she had to keep eating something. It had been empty for so long, it actually physically hurt to eat. The water the soldier had given her was the best she'd ever had. She watched as Julie gulped hers down, but Fiona savored hers. It wasn't cold, not even close, and it wasn't designer, but it was clean, and that was a huge step up from what she had been drinking. Fiona didn't feel any grit in her mouth after drinking it and while it had a slightly metallic taste from whatever cleansing tablet the soldier used to make sure it was clean and healthy, it still tasted awesome.

It was easier for Fiona to take her time eating the granola bar when Julie and the man weren't watching her every move. Fiona had no idea what his name was, he hadn't told them. She desperately wanted to call him something other than "the man" or "the soldier" in her head, but she thought it'd be rude to outright ask him. Fiona suddenly had a thought. If he was a Navy SEAL she probably shouldn't even be calling him "soldier." Didn't they call themselves "sailors," or was it "seamen"? Damn. Fiona's head hurt. If he wanted to let them know what his name was, he'd tell them. Maybe he wasn't even allowed to tell them. Maybe it was some top secret thing that SEALs weren't allowed to tell the people they rescued who they were.

Fiona knew her brain was flitting from one subject to the other with no rhyme or reason, but she couldn't help it. She was hanging onto her sanity by a thread. All she wanted to do was drop to the ground and curl into a little ball, close her eyes, wiggle her nose, and find herself back in her apartment in El Paso…but she couldn't. Of course she couldn't. Fiona had sworn to the soldier that she wouldn't be any trouble. She could hang on for a bit longer…maybe.

Her hands still shook, and Fiona's body's craving for whatever drugs she'd been given was still there, but as long as she could concentrate on something other than having more of the toxic cocktail injected into her body, she could stave off the drug withdrawal reaction just a bit longer. Fiona didn't want the man to know what was happening. He'd certainly leave her behind then. He had to get Julie out of there and back to the States. Or maybe he'd decide they shouldn't continue on if she just stopped on the trail, and that wasn't acceptable. Fiona wanted out of this jungle. She could hold on just a little bit more. It wasn't that far until they'd get to where he said someone would come and pick them up.

They'd been walking for what seemed like a long time, but after a while the man stopped and signaled for she and Julie to crouch down in a clump of trees. Fiona sensed something was wrong. She watched the soldier closely. He hadn't said anything, but he looked tense. He was crouched down beside them and there was a cleared section of the forest just beyond the trees. It wasn't quiet, there were too many animal noises for it to be called silent in the forest, but Fiona still thought it was eerie…obviously the soldier did too.

He kept looking at his watch and up at the sky. Fiona figured their transportation was late, or wasn't coming. She absently scratched a bite on her leg with shaking fingers. Her withdrawal symptoms were getting worse. If they didn't get out of here, he was going to notice. Fiona didn't know what he'd do. Leave her? Be disgusted? Get pissed at her? She couldn't risk telling him. She'd just have to ride it through, just like everything else she'd gone through.

"What are we waiting for?" Julie whined softly. "My

butt hurts and I want to go home."

Cookie sighed. Shit. When things went bad, they did it in grand style.

He turned toward the women. Julie had crocodile tears running down her face and Fiona just stared at him as if she knew he was going to say something was wrong.

"Change of plans," he said bluntly, making his decision. "The helicopter didn't show and I can't get through to my teammates. We have to move to the back-up extraction point."

Cookie knew some people would assume the team was just running late, but SEALs didn't "run late." Something was wrong and it was time to move to the backup plan they'd rehearsed before the mission started. Cookie deliberately didn't tell the women where the backup extraction point was, but Julie wasn't having any of his vague explanations.

"But where is it? How much further do we have to go? I thought we were going to be picked up here."

Julie's voice was whiney and it grated on Cookie's last nerve. He held on to his temper by the skin of his teeth. He was used to having his team with him as a buffer. Anytime a rescued person became too much, they'd take turns with the person. He missed his team. Cookie always preferred working with his friends than by himself. It was how the SEALs normally operated and this mission was making it clear to Cookie, once again, why. He was having a hard time dealing with Julie.

He sighed and scrubbed his face with one of his hands. "It's a ways away, but we don't have to get there today. We have a few days…"

Cookie was interrupted by Julie. "A few days?" she screeched too loudly for the quiet jungle. "What the hell are you talking about? I thought you were here to rescue me, we need to get out of mmph…"

Cookie moved quickly for a man with a huge pack on his back. His hand was over Julie's mouth before the last syllable came out.

"Shhhhh," he ordered furiously. "The men who kidnapped you could be anywhere. Besides them, this jungle is crawling with drug runners and other men we definitely don't want to run into. We aren't safe here. You need to remember that and keep it down." Cookie watched as Julie nodded fearfully, her eyes wide.

Fiona could see the solider was upset. The entire rescue had been full of surprises, and not good ones. The least of which was her presence, and now apparently their ride hadn't arrived. She wanted to reassure the man, but wasn't sure what to say, so she kept silent.

Cookie slowly removed his hand from Julie's mouth. "Here's the plan. We'll walk south toward the river, then double back again and head west. They'll figure that we'll follow the river, so we'll do the opposite. Just stay close to me and you'll be fine," he said to Julie, knowing he didn't have to tell Fiona to stick close. He knew she'd do it or die trying.

Cookie glanced at Fiona. She hadn't taken her eyes off of him and something eased inside him with her calm acceptance of the situation. At least he wouldn't have two hysterical women to deal with. He gave Fiona what he hoped was a reassuring nod and said, "Let's go."

Cookie had no idea where Mozart was, he couldn't reach him on the satellite radio and obviously something had gone wrong with the helicopter, otherwise Dude and Benny would've been there by now. It could be that they had to pick Mozart up because he ran into trouble. Whatever the reason was, Cookie didn't waste time dwelling on it. The team had made the alternate arrangements for pick up for just this reason. Sometimes things just didn't go as planned and they'd have to adjust their plans.

The trio headed back into the jungle. They had a long way to go before they were safe.

Julie had finally ceased complaining about an hour before they stopped for the night. Cookie figured she had the right to be tired, but they were all in the same boat...actually they weren't. He glanced at Fiona. He hadn't heard her say anything for a while. She'd kept quiet and had kept up with them, as she'd promised. He could only wish Julie had the same inner fortitude as

Fiona did.

Cookie didn't know how long Fiona had been in captivity, but he was certain it was a hell of a lot longer than Julie had been. He knew something was up with her, but he hadn't had the time to figure it out...until now.

They'd stopped and Julie had immediately sat on the ground and brought her knees up to her chest and clasped her hands around them. She laid her head on her knees and hadn't moved as he set up their make-shift camp for the night. It wasn't much; they couldn't afford to light a fire, possibly alerting anyone lurking in the dark jungle where they were. Cookie recalled the short conversation he'd had with Fiona as they'd settled in. She'd asked if she could help him in any way. He'd thanked her, but told her honestly that she'd just slow him down. She hadn't pouted or sulked; she'd just nodded, as if she'd expected his response, and sat against a nearby tree, out of his way.

He'd talk to her now that they were stopped for the night. It hadn't been a big deal to set up three lean-tos instead of the two that he'd planned. Supplies were plentiful in the jungle, leaves and sticks. Cookie was traveling light and didn't have any tents. He hadn't thought he'd need them in the first place, but even if he'd planned on spending several nights in the jungle, he preferred to keep his pack as light as possible, and tents would've added quite a bit of weight. Cookie had handed out another granola bar to each of the women, and had heated up two Meals Ready to Eat. They'd all split the food, with Fiona only eating a little bit, claiming her stomach hurt from the heavy food that she wasn't used to, and now both women were resting.

Cookie looked over at Fiona now. She was still propped up by the tree with her arms around her legs. Her head was resting on her knees and her eyes were closed. She was in much the same position as Julie had been, but somehow she looked more vulnerable than Julie had.

Cookie thought again as to what was "off" about Fiona. Was it her feet? They were pretty beat up. Had she been hurt by the branches and shit they'd walked through? She wasn't wearing pants. Maybe the men had hurt her last night before he'd gotten there. Shit, she had to have been raped and was probably scared to be around him.

That last thought made Cookie visibly flinch and feel physically sick. He'd been around rape victims before, but for some reason this time was different. Maybe it was because he was the only one around. Maybe it was because Fiona was trying so hard to be brave. Whatever it was, all Cookie knew was that something inside him completely rebelled at the thought of her being violated that way.

Unfortunately, they had about ten more miles to walk before they'd get to the second extraction point. Ten fucking miles. They had two more days to get there, which meant two more days of hard walking. If someone had told him he'd have to have two kidnapped women hike over ten miles through the Mexican jungle, he'd have told them they were crazy. But here they were. Cookie wasn't sure either woman would make it, and that worried him.

Julie was the stronger of the two, but she was soft. She wasn't used to the exercise and she complained every step of the way. It was obvious in her "real" life, anytime something was "hard," she was allowed to quit. Not able to keep the mean thought out of his head, Cookie wasn't sure *he'd* make it another two days if he had to listen to Julie's incessant complaints the entire time.

He thought Fiona should be able to make it, but he wasn't positive. If she'd been at one hundred percent, Cookie had no doubt she would've made the ten mile hike look easy. Hell, she probably could've done it in a day. But she *wasn't* a hundred percent. Hell, she probably wasn't even at fifty percent. She'd been captive a hell of a lot longer than Julie, and she didn't look good. But she hadn't given up. She'd soldiered on all day without one word of complaint. Cookie was fucking impressed.

The flip flops Fiona was wearing worried him. Fuck,

who was he kidding, everything about her worried Cookie. Her lack of long pants, the collar around her neck, her shaking hands, her dehydration, her obvious hunger…Cookie needed to find out what was going on with her tonight, so he could make better decisions for all of them.

Once Julie was settled for the night, Cookie walked over to where Fiona was sitting. She was still resting against the tree silently. If Cookie didn't see her back lightly moving up and down he would've been afraid she was dead. As he walked up to her she opened her eyes, but didn't otherwise move. Cookie sat down beside her.

"How are you holding up?" Cookie asked quietly.

"I'm fine," Fiona told him. "I won't slow you down."

Cookie nodded and told her, "I know, you've done great so far." He paused, then continued. "I don't think I've introduced myself to you yet. I'm Cookie." He didn't bother reaching out his hand for her to shake. They'd gone beyond the social niceties.

"Cookie?" Fiona stared at the handsome man sitting next to her trying to make small talk. She felt like crying. He was trying to make her feel normal, and she appreciated it more than she could say.

"Yeah, everyone on my team has a nickname. There's Dude, Mozart, Wolf, Abe, Benny, and me…Cookie."

"Are you going to tell me why you're called Cookie?"

"Are you gonna laugh if I do?"

Fiona loved the easy-going banter. Hell, just hearing someone talk to her in English felt awesome. "Probably. Especially since you seem to be reluctant to tell me."

Cookie chuckled. He knew it was inappropriate, but he was enjoying the hell out of this conversation, especially after the tension and complaining from Julie all day. He'd obviously taken too long to respond because Fiona continued talking.

"Are you going to make me guess?"

"You'd never guess, Fee."

Fiona jerked her head off her knees to look at him. What had he called her?

"What? You think you *can* guess?" Cookie had noticed her reaction, and correctly guessed it was in a result of him calling her "Fee." He didn't know where it came from, but it sounded right in his head. She looked like a "Fee."

"Uh, okay, your mom sent you cookies every week while you were in basic training?"

"I went to boot camp, not basic. And good guess, but no. Strike one." Cookie watched as Fiona's eyes narrowed. She obviously had a competitive spirit. He'd have to remember that and use it to keep her going later if he had to.

"When you were little, you ate too many cookies one Christmas and puked your guts out?"

A low surprised laugh escaped from between Cookie's lips before he could keep it back. "Wow, I think I'm hurt. Nope, that's not it either. One more guess left."

Fiona's whole body hurt, she was exhausted and thirstier than she could ever remember being, but for some reason she was having fun. This man had surprised her. She thought he'd be all business and gruff, but she liked this side of him. Let's see...why would someone have the nickname Cookie? Fiona decided to really mess with him. What the hell, she had nothing to lose.

"You were a virgin when you joined the Navy and after *boot camp* your buddies took you out on the town and paid an eighty year old whore named Cookie to deflower you."

Cookie started laughing, quietly, and couldn't stop. It was several moments before he could speak.

"Jesus, Fee, I'll have to remember not to piss you off in the future. First, I was *deflowered* when I was fourteen by my seventeen-year-old date to the Homecoming Dance. So, your last guess is also wrong. Although you're much more creative than what the reason for my nickname really is. I was the last member to join the team. Typically newbies are called nuggets, FNGs, or cookies. Cookie stuck."

They sat there for a moment just looking at each other.

Not knowing what a "FNG" was, Fiona decided to let it go. It didn't really matter anyway. "Do you have a real name?" Fiona didn't know why she wanted to know, but she did.

"Hunter. Hunter Knox."

"Are you serious?"

"Dead. Why?"

Fiona couldn't believe that was really his name. "Because it's the kind of name a stripper or superhero would have." She immediately blushed. Oh crap. Had she really just said that out loud? Jesus, she was *such* a dork.

"I think I'll take that as a compliment, Fee, but I prefer to strip for a party of one."

"Please, just ignore me. I don't know what I'm saying. Let me try again." Fiona looked up. She was embarrassed, but determined to say it. "It's nice to meet you, Hunter. No, it's fucking *awesome* to meet you. I've never been so glad to meet anyone in my entire life."

Cookie's eyes lost their humor and he got serious immediately. He understood what she was saying. "I'm happier to have met you than anyone I've met in *my* entire life, Fee."

A comfortable silence fell between them. Fiona put her head back on her knees, and closed her eyes again.

Noticing her white knuckles from squeezing her hands tightly Cookie finally asked what had been on his mind for most of the day. "I need to know what's up, Fee." He watched as she flinched. "I don't know what's going through your head, but I'm not going to leave you. I'm not going to get mad, I just need to know so I can be sure we all get through this and get home. If your feet are bothering you, I can wrap them with tape to help with that. Shit, I should've already done it. We can coat your legs with mud to try to protect them a bit more. I can see all the welts from the bug bites. I wish I had an extra pair of pants for you."

Fiona didn't say anything, just continued to sit next to him silently. Cookie was frustrated. He wanted to help her, but he couldn't if she wouldn't talk to him. Finally, he thought he knew what to say to get Fiona to open up to him. Cookie knew she was stubborn and tough just from being around her for a day and for surviving her kidnapping ordeal. He thought of what he could say that would get to her. Finally he knew. It'd be the same thing that, if said to him, would get him to open up and be honest.

Cookie lowered his voice and spoke from his heart. "No bullshit, Fiona, my life depends on you. I will *not* leave you. If I don't know what's going on with you, and you fall behind or can't continue, that could end up hurting me as well, because I'll stay with you and try to help you. There's no way in hell I've brought you this far to leave you behind now. You're stuck with me. No matter what."

He waited. Cookie thought maybe Fiona had fallen asleep or that she was going to refuse to talk to him.

Finally Fiona spoke softly, without opening her eyes. "I'm going through withdrawal."

Chapter Five

WHATEVER COOKIE THOUGHT Fiona was going to say, it wasn't that.

"What?" he asked more harshly than he'd intended. His mind whirled. How could he have missed that? Cookie couldn't believe it. Well, it was dark in the room he'd found her in and she was now wearing a long sleeve shirt, so he'd never gotten a good look at her arms.

Fiona kept her eyes closed and continued, "They'd been shooting me up with something. I'm not sure what. Not enough to freak me out, but enough to control me, to keep me complacent. I think they thought they could get me to do what they wanted if they got me hooked, that I'd do anything for another fix. But I refused to beg or behave for them. It's been a while since they last gave me anything, I don't know for sure how long. I swear if it gets bad enough, that if I slow you down, I'll let you go ahead. I know you didn't bargain on this, or me...I'm sorry. I'm so sorry. I should've told you before we left that hut." Fiona's voice trailed off. She'd kept her eyes closed throughout her entire confession. Fiona waited for Hunter to get up and walk away in disgust. Not only was she disgusting and filthy and smelly, she was an addict too.

Cookie swallowed once. He had to swallow again before he could talk. He was relieved it wasn't something more serious on one hand, but at the same time, he knew sometimes getting off of drugs was the worst part. He knew what he said now was important.

"Can I see?" Cookie waited, and when Fiona nodded slightly, moved so he was kneeling in front of her. He gently unclasped her hands and took hold of one and threaded his fingers with hers. Cookie waited until Fiona opened her eyes to check on what he was doing.

He kept eye contact with her while he pushed the sleeve on her right arm up past her elbow. It wasn't until it was all the way up that he looked down. He clenched his teeth at the needle marks inside her elbow. He could clearly see them, even with the waning light of the evening. He lowered that sleeve, and pushed up the other one to see the same thing. The bruising on her arms was an indication of how she'd fought her captors and how they hadn't been gentle when injecting her.

Cookie smoothed her shirt down and took both her hands in his. Fiona was watching him now warily. He could feel the tremors in her hands.

He met her eyes and said, "Fee, I'm so sorry. I'm

sorry I didn't get there quicker. I'm sorry I didn't know you were there. I'm just so damn sorry."

When Fiona took a breath ready to say something, Cookie interrupted her. "No, don't say anything, and *don't* fucking apologize again. Listen to me. I've only known you for a day, but you're one of the strongest people I know. Not just the strongest *woman* I know, but one of the strongest *people*. You haven't told me how long you were in that damn building, but I know it was a while. You've walked a shit ton of miles today, on your own, without complaint. I don't know how long it's been since you've had something decent to eat or drink. All you care about is this mission and not being in the way. You are *not* in the way. If there were ten women in that hovel, I would've rescued all of them, even though I was only expecting one."

Cookie paused and let his comment sink in, then continued, "We have two more days of hard walking. We only have two days before our next scheduled backup pickup. I obviously don't have anything to give you to help you with the withdrawal. Without knowing exactly what drugs they were giving you, I don't want to risk injecting you with the wrong thing. I've got some pain killers in my pack, but it's not a good idea to mix them with unknown narcotics. While I don't have anything to counteract your withdrawal symptoms, I can certainly help distract you or do anything else you think will help. Okay? Don't shut me out." Then Cookie chuckled and pleaded softly, humor coating his words, "Please don't leave me with Julie as my only conversation."

Fiona smiled at his words, but sobered quickly, staring at Hunter with big eyes, her concern and worry clearly showing.

Cookie continued on. "I'm not a therapist and I can't imagine what you've been through, but if you need someone to talk to…"

Fiona nodded, cutting Hunter off. She knew she'd never tell him what she'd survived. It'd been bad enough to have gone through it; she couldn't bear for him to feel any more sorry for her then he already did. She liked Hunter. Genuinely liked him. She hadn't known many military people, but she imagined them all to be either grunting, sex-hungry jerks or assholes who thought they were more important than anyone around them. Obviously she'd been stereotyping, because Hunter wasn't either. At least she didn't think so. He'd sounded genuinely concerned for her. That concern felt wonderful.

Cookie squeezed her hand. "Try to get some sleep, Fee. We'll be starting off early tomorrow. I want to get going before it gets too hot. And remember, I'm here if you need to talk."

Fiona squeezed his hand back and then dropped it

to clasp her legs again. She couldn't rely on him. She knew she'd probably be out of her head before too much longer, and she had to concentrate to keep herself under control. She scooted into the little lean to Hunter had made for her without saying anything else and curled into a ball. Fiona could tell she was getting worse. Her captors had never let her go this long before. She knew Hunter said he'd help, but there was nothing he could do. Fiona needed to distract herself; she started counting backward from one thousand again.

At four the next morning, Cookie woke the women up. Each got another granola bar and he checked their water. He eyed Fiona warily. She didn't look good. She refused to look him in the eyes, and the tremors in her hands were worse, even though she tried to hide it from him. She was also very pale. She ate the granola bar with the same enjoyment she had the day before, just as Julie ate hers with the same disgust. When they were done, and had relieved themselves in the bushes nearby, they set off.

The heat was brutal. The fact they weren't walking near the river meant they didn't have to worry as much about animals who'd go there to drink, but it also meant they had to conserve what water they had. It also meant that it was hot; hotter than it might have been if they'd been able to cool off with a dip in the fast flowing water now and then.

Julie didn't talk much, but when she did, it was to whine about how much further they had to go and how hot she was. She also complained about her feet hurting, the bugs, the leaves smacking her in the face…the list was endless. But Fiona was quiet. Too quiet. She trudged along behind Julie without a word. Cookie looked back to check on her often and saw Fiona was making it…barely. He knew she was weak, but now knowing about the drugs her captors had forced on her, he was even more concerned.

When they stopped for a short food break, Fiona uncharacteristically laid down in the shade of a tree and curled into a ball, her preferred resting stance now. Cookie was busy with his pack and didn't notice until Julie groaned sarcastically, "Oh great, we'll never get there now."

Cookie saw Fiona start to sit up upon hearing Julie's words. He went over and put his hand on her back.

"Stay. Rest. We'll get going soon enough." He looked at Julie and said in a harsh tone, without bothering to try to tone it down. "You should lie down and take a nap too. We've still got some ground to cover today."

Fiona looked up at Hunter with misery in her eyes as he turned back toward her. "I'm sorry."

Cookie cut her off. "None of that. Shit, Fiona, you aren't superwoman. Just rest a bit and we'll leave in a while. And before you say it, you aren't holding us up. We all need a break and it's safe enough."

Fiona nodded and squeezed her eyes shut again. She heard Hunter walk away. She knew he was probably lying for her sake, but she couldn't make herself care at the moment. Fiona felt like crap. Her whole body was rebelling against her. She wished those damn kidnappers were there to give her the drugs. She was ready to beg for them now. She'd finally gotten to the point where she'd do whatever they wanted in order to get them. Fiona knew they were bad, even without knowing exactly what crap they'd been shoving into her body, but she'd do anything to get rid of the crawling sensation under her skin and the horrible nausea.

The shakes she could deal with, but the feeling of bugs crawling on her was horrible. She itched something fierce as well, but she tried to resist the urge to scratch. Fiona knew that once she started she wouldn't stop. Hell, half of the itch was probably from bug bites and not from the drugs, but it didn't matter right now. Itchy was itchy.

Fiona choked back a sob. Why hadn't they killed her? Why? They had the chance. More than once. She couldn't think straight. She took a deep breath. She had to stop thinking that way. She knew Hunter wouldn't leave her in the jungle, and if he wouldn't leave her, then none of them would get out anytime soon, maybe not at all. She couldn't live with that on her conscience. Fiona took a deep breath to get herself together and not give in to the despair desperately trying to suck her down and started counting backward...this time from two thousand.

Cookie watched Fiona. She wasn't sleeping. He could see her lips moving. He finally realized she was counting. Around the same time he figured it out, he heard Julie say with malice, "That's all she did when we were in that fucking building. She counted backwards. It nearly drove me crazy."

Cookie just looked at Julie incredulously. She couldn't really be that callous could she?

"Well? It did!" Julie retorted defensively after seeing the look on Cookie's face, but fell silent under his continued scathing glare.

Yup, she could be that callous. Finally Cookie knew they couldn't wait any longer. It was time to move. He stood up and was going to go over to help Fiona, but he saw she was sitting up on her own. She'd heard him moving around and knew it was time to go. The pitiful little group gathered up their belongings and started out again.

A couple of hours later, Fiona started dry heaving. She didn't have any food in her stomach to really throw up, other than a few bites of granola, but her body tried to get rid of anything that was there anyway. She stopped in the middle of the path and dry heaved. She'd tried to stop it, but it was impossible. The retching noises she made were horrifying.

Julie screeched and jumped out of the way yelling, "Gross!"

While Cookie wasn't sorry he'd rescued Julie, she was a human being, and a woman at that, he *was* wishing she'd just be quiet for one fucking second. She was obviously spoiled and wasn't dealing with the logistics of being rescued that well. Cookie didn't analyze his thoughts too much. He'd probably had former captives act worse than Julie was, but when he compared Julie's actions to Fiona's, he was hard pressed to have much sympathy toward Julie.

Cookie went to Fiona. She held out her hand as if to ward him off, but he just took her hand and kept coming. He led her away from where Julie was standing and just held her upright as her stomach spasmed.

Fiona was so embarrassed. She wanted nothing more than to lie down on the jungle floor and die, but she couldn't. She took a deep breath, and with Hunter's strength straightened.

"I'm okay," she whispered. "We need to keep going."

"Jesus, Fee, just rest for a second. I've got you."

Fiona would've cried if she had any extra liquid in her body. She stood, shaking, with her side against

Hunter. He was holding her sideways in case she had to throw up again, but she knew she was done...for the moment.

Cookie pulled away, just enough, so that he could lean over and look in Fiona's eyes. "I wish like hell I could take this for you."

Fiona could only say quietly, "I wouldn't wish this on my worst enemy."

Cookie ran his hand over Fiona's head and smoothed her hair down. Without a word he leaned over and kissed her lightly on the top of the head before asking quietly, "Ready?"

Fiona nodded briefly, deciding she couldn't deal with understanding Hunter's actions right then. Maybe later she'd remember his touch and his kiss and analyze it. But for now, she had to concentrate on staying upright and mobile. For Hunter's sake.

Cookie knew Fiona was right when she'd said they had to keep going, but he wasn't happy about it. She needed a medical care, immediately. But that wasn't going to happen anytime soon. He hadn't meant to kiss her, but he been unable to control himself. Cookie wanted to take Fiona in his arms and whisk her away, but it was impossible. He'd consoled himself with the caress of his hand and the brief kiss.

When they started off again, Cookie walked beside Fiona, this time with his arm around her waist. He had to stop with her several more times as she dry heaved. Finally Cookie calculated they'd walked far enough for the day. They were mostly on track to get to the extraction point on time, and he stopped to let them all settle for the night. They'd made his goal of five miles, but he'd secretly hoped they'd get further so they'd have less to go tomorrow.

When Cookie had Julie settled, thank God she wasn't trying to cling to him, and was satisfied they were as safe as they could be for the moment, he went to join Fiona. She hadn't moved much since he'd helped her to the ground, and he was worried about her.

She also hadn't eaten anything, not wanting, in her words, to "waste it" by throwing it up as soon as she ate it. Cookie didn't know what it was that made him want to be by Fiona's side, well, actually he *did* know. It was her courage and inner strength.

Cookie had seen it before, with Caroline. When Wolf's woman had been kidnapped by terrorists and thrown overboard in the middle of the ocean with her feet tied together and weighted down, he'd been the one to get to her and give her lifesaving oxygen while Wolf and the team took down the terrorists. Cookie had been amazed at Caroline's fortitude and strength then, and still was today. He hadn't met anyone like her, until Fiona.

Cookie had promised himself that if he *did* meet

someone like Caroline, he'd snatch her up and never let her go. When Cookie made that silent vow to himself, he hadn't expected to actually find a woman he admired as much as he admired Caroline. But it wasn't admiration, exactly, he was feeling about Fiona.

Cookie had been on hostage recovery missions that were way worse than this one. Bullets flying was the worst, but most of the time they were hard because of the lack of inner fortitude of the person, or people, being rescued. Cookie and the team never blamed them, after all, being kidnapped wasn't ever a good experience, but the fact that this woman, held longer than anyone he'd ever rescued before, was dealing with a reaction to a withdrawal of some sort of drug, and knew she was only being rescued because someone else had been sent for….it made him respect her. Respect and pride. That was what he was feeling about this woman.

There were very few people in his life that Cookie truly respected. The fact that he'd known Fiona for two days and respected her said a lot. He was also fucking proud of her. Fiona was holding her own in a horrible situation. She deserved a fucking medal. Cookie eased down beside her.

Fiona was on her side curled into a ball, as usual. The woman stunk to high heaven, was covered in dirt and filth, and was wearing a metal collar around her neck. Cookie wanted to get as close as he could to her to offer comfort, regardless of all that. To let her know she wasn't alone. He supposed that he shouldn't do it, especially with Julie shooting daggers at them from across the way, but he couldn't help but offer this woman comfort.

Fiona felt Hunter ease himself onto the ground beside her and fit himself around her. His front to her back. He didn't try to move her, she was still curled into a protective ball, but she fit in the crook of his body better than she thought she ever would with a man. Fiona was pretty tall for a woman, around five nine, and had never found a man that had "fit" her as Hunter had.

Fiona knew that Hunter could feel her trembling, but she couldn't stop it.

Cookie felt helpless. He was a Navy SEAL. He could solve almost any problem thrown his way. He could fight the meanest bad guy, swim the widest ocean, fall from the sky and come out shooting, but he couldn't do anything for the woman trembling in his arms. Not one fucking thing. The only thing he could do for her was talk to her.

"You're doing fine, Fee."

Fiona shook her head in denial. "I don't think I'm going to make it, Hunter," she whispered, scared if she said it too loud, it'd somehow make it true.

"Are you kidding me? You've already made it."

"What are you talking about? Did you eat a bad

SUSAN STOKER

mushroom at some point in the last day?" Fiona tried to joke with Hunter. If she didn't make a joke, she'd probably cry.

Cookie ran his hand over Fiona's head, wiping the sweat off her forehead in the process. "Funny girl. I mean, you've already made it away from those jackasses. *That* was the hard part. *This* is a piece of cake."

Fiona closed her eyes and whispered her greatest fear out loud. "What if I freak out and get you killed?"

Cookie's heart about broke in his chest. Fiona hadn't said, "What if I freak out and they take me back," she'd been more concerned about him. Jesus fucking Christ.

"You won't freak out, Fee."

"You don't know that."

Cookie turned her head just enough and got up on an elbow so he could look into Fiona's eyes. "I know we've just met, but I know you. You'll hold on until we're safe. I *know* you will." Cookie watched as Fiona closed her eyes, but continued anyway, keeping his hand on her face, liking the connection it gave him to her. "And even if you don't hold on, and you *do* freak out, you won't get me killed and I won't allow them to take you back. I swear."

"Don't get hurt on account of me, Hunter. You're so much more valuable than I am."

Cookie couldn't take it anymore. Every time he

70

tried to reassure Fiona, she turned around and said something else that slayed him.

"Shhhh, Fee. Rest. You're safe. Just relax."

They laid on the ground for a while longer. Cookie knew Fee wasn't sleeping. "What do you count to?" he asked her unexpectedly.

"What?" Fiona stammered, feeling embarrassed. She hadn't realized Hunter had heard her counting. It was the one thing that had kept her sane in the pit they'd held her in, but now it was the *only* thing that kept her from falling into hysterics with the withdrawal.

"I know you've been counting to distract yourself," Cookie said softly. "Let me help."

"Really, Hunter," Fiona complained, "you should get some rest…I smell horrible, you have other things to worry about…"

Cookie cut her off. "What do you count to?" His words were hard and unrelenting.

Fiona sighed to herself. She didn't know how Hunter counting would distract her, but she finally told him. "I usually start at one thousand and count backwards, but lately I've been starting at two thousand."

Cookie said nothing, but leaned down and kissed her temple, holding his lips against her skin for a moment. Then he brought his lips to her ear and softly started counting. "Two thousand, One thousand nine hundred ninety nine, one thousand nine hundred ninety eight…"

Fiona counted in her head with him, loving the low, rumbly sound of Hunter's voice. It was deep and soft and soothing. Her exhausted body soon fell into a troubled sleep with the sound of Hunter's voice still counting in her head.

Chapter Six

THE NEXT MORNING Cookie woke up early again. He enjoyed the feel of Fiona in his arms, even in their present not-so-good situation. He hated to wake her up and that they had another tough day of trekking through the jungle. Fiona had just about broken his heart last night with her words. She was trying desperately to hold on and be brave, but Cookie could tell she was struggling.

The situation wasn't ideal. Fiona wasn't at her best, hell that was the understatement of the year, but Cookie was still drawn to her. Even smelly, sweaty, covered in dirt, and suffering from withdrawal from who-the-hell-knew what drugs, Cookie thought she was amazing. He gently eased off the ground and removed his arm from around Fiona's waist and got up. Cookie slid a lock of hair off Fiona's cheek and tucked it behind her ear gently, then turned to get ready for the day. Knowing they had one more day of grueling travel before they could reach the extraction point, Cookie wanted to let the women sleep longer before having to wake them.

After stalling as late as possible, Cookie finally woke them up. Julie was irritable and had no problem letting Cookie know it. She bitched about the hard ground, the lack of good food, even about not having a damn toilet. Cookie ignored her as much as he could. He only had to get through one more day before she'd be someone else's issue. It was a terrible thing to think after what she'd been through, but he couldn't help it.

Once Fiona was up and moving, Cookie thought she actually looked a bit better than the day before, but she still in no way looked good. He could still see her hands shaking. She was able to keep half of a granola bar down and Cookie took that as a good sign. He was running low on food, but hopefully it wouldn't make a difference after tonight. There was no way Cookie was letting Fiona know they had just one more granola bar left. She'd insist that he or Julie eat it, when it was obvious she was the one who needed the nutrients the most.

Fiona was glad she'd been able to eat something and not immediately throw it back up; she hoped she was coming out on the other side of the worst of the withdrawal symptoms she'd been experiencing, but she wasn't sure. She still smelled horrible and most likely looked like a refugee from a third world country. Fiona was glad she hadn't seen a mirror. She didn't think she wanted to see her reflection anytime in her near future. She was covered in bug bites as well. They were maddeningly itchy. Her feet were not faring well in the flip-flops either, but Fiona knew she had no choice there. Hunter had tried to wrap them in tape before they set off yesterday, but the tape would only last so long. She had blisters between her first and second toes because of the plastic on the flip flops between them, but honestly, they were the least of her problems at the moment. Fiona purposely hadn't asked Hunter how long they had to walk today, not wanting to know.

After their lunch break, Cookie told the women they were coming to the most dangerous part of their trip. There was a reason this was Plan B. First, it was a lot further from the kidnapper's camp, but second it was in a more populated area and near a well-known drug runner's hangout. They all had to keep quiet and not talk unless absolutely necessary. Cookie told them to watch where they were walking and try to make as little sound as possible. He didn't think they'd have to worry about the kidnappers finding them this far out, but the last thing he wanted to happen was to run into drug runners while escaping from sex traffickers.

Finally, after a long quiet couple of hours of walking, Cookie stopped. "Okay, ladies, here's the plan," he told them quietly. "The chopper should be here in about an hour. We need to sit tight and wait. You can rest and get your strength back as much as possible. Be ready for anything when the chopper comes into range. If anything happens, and I mean *anything*, you two are to get your butts to that chopper. I'll cover your backs and make sure you get there. Got it?"

Julie, not surprisingly, nodded enthusiastically, agreeing to anything as long as it got her out of the jungle. Fiona wasn't as quick to agree. Somehow Cookie knew she'd protest.

Fiona had been feeling better earlier, but started feeling shaky again when they stopped to wait for the helicopter. She didn't like what Hunter was saying and let him know in no uncertain terms. "No, not okay," she said defiantly.

"Shut up," Julie hissed meanly, not waiting for Cookie to say anything. "He's here because of *me*, if it wasn't for *me*, you wouldn't even have been rescued. So let him rescue us and shut the hell up!"

Fiona looked at Julie incredulously. "You're right; if not for Hunter, *you'd* still be in that stinking building or on your way to be some guy's sex toy. You're willing to let him *die* for you?"

Without waiting for an answer, to what was obviously a rhetorical question, Fiona turned to Hunter. "There's no way we've come this far to leave you behind now. Tell us what to be on the lookout for and we can help you."

Cookie shook his head and kept his voice even, yet firm. He couldn't deny it felt good to have Fiona stand up for him, even if he didn't need it. Not many women had the guts to go to bat for him. At least none in the recent past that he could remember.

"No, Fiona, that isn't how this works. I'm the professional, you're not. You'll follow my orders and get on that chopper, no questions asked. I can deal with any situation that arises here. I'm a Navy SEAL, a professional soldier. If I know you're safe I can concentrate better and I'll be better off without the two of you here."

His words hurt, but Fiona knew Hunter spoke nothing but the truth. She didn't want to give up her argument though.

At the stubborn look in her eye, Cookie eased his voice a bit. "Fee, this isn't my first mission. I know what I'm doing. Even if for some reason I can't get on the chopper, I know what to do. I'll dig in and hang out until my team can come back and get me. And they *will* come back to get me. A SEAL doesn't leave a SEAL behind, ever. It's much easier for just me to hide and wait them out than it would be if I have to look after you or Julie as well."

Fiona heard what Hunter was saying, but she didn't like it. Well, Hunter could say what he wanted; she wasn't going to leave him in the jungle if she could help it, even if his team would come back for him. Fiona knew what it was like to be left behind, and she swore she wouldn't put anyone else through it, ever.

Time ticked by slowly. The hour they had to wait was one of the longest hours of Fiona's life. Finally, *finally,* they heard the faint sound of a helicopter.

"Come on," was all Cookie said. He started off through the jungle, hacking the branches away from their path as he went. He wasn't trying to be quiet, he was trying to get them to the landing zone as quickly as possible.

"It's about a quarter of a mile through the trees, straight line distance, this way," he'd told them earlier pointing toward the west. "No problem."

It *was* a problem though. As soon as they heard the chopper, obviously so did the drug runners. While they didn't know exactly where it was headed, they had a pretty good guess since there weren't very many places it could land or get close to the ground in the area.

When Cookie, Julie, and Fiona finally reached the area where they were to be picked up, all hell broke loose. The drug runners had reached the area at the same time and easily spotted them and opened fire. Cookie didn't hesitate and returned fire. The loud sound of gunfire startled Fiona.

The noise was extremely loud compared to the si-lence they'd been traveling in. Cookie's teammates in the chopper began laying down cover fire. They signaled to Cookie and he urged Julie and Fiona toward a small opening in the trees. It was going to be tricky. They had to climb onto a lowered ladder and be hauled up. The chopper couldn't land, and they were going to be sitting ducks while they were being hauled aboard.

Julie went first. Cookie and Fiona kneeled down in a patch of thick bushes. Cookie was firing toward where he thought the drug runners were hiding in the jungle around them. He'd taken off his pack to have better range of motion.

It was taking a while for Julie to grab a hold of the ladder. Fiona wanted to scream in frustration. Why didn't she just grab the damn thing and get the hell out of there? Cookie was running out of ammo, he didn't have an unlimited amount of bullets. They both knew if he had to stop firing, Julie could be injured.

Cookie was surprised, but supposed he shouldn't have been, when he heard Fiona say, "Here," and thrust his original pistol at him, fully loaded again. She'd loaded it while he was firing his backup. Cookie didn't say anything, simply grabbed it and started shooting again.

Fiona re-loaded the pistol Hunter had just emptied. Her hands were shaking badly, so it was a tough job, but she knew Hunter had to concentrate or else they were all dead. She knew how to load and shoot pistols because in her world back in El Paso, she'd decided she needed to be proactive for her own self-protection. She lived alone and wanted to be sure she could handle a gun to protect herself. She'd taken gun safety lessons and actually owned a pistol herself. That simple decision she'd made so long ago was certainly paying off now.

Finally Julie was up safe in the chopper. Fiona hadn't watched her go up; she'd been concentrating on loading the bullets into the gun. It was probably a good thing. If she'd watched, it might've scared the crap out of her.

Suddenly it was Fiona's turn. Without a word, Cookie went to push her forward to take her turn, when suddenly he fell backward.

Fiona looked down in horror. Hunter was lying still on the ground with blood coming from somewhere around his upper chest. He'd been shot!

Fiona looked around quickly and made a split second decision. Hunter was going to live, dammit. He certainly didn't deserve to die out here in the fucking jungle. He'd risked his life for Julie, and for her, and she wasn't going to save herself and leave him here. Fiona knew she'd never be able to live with herself if she just up and left Hunter bleeding on the ground. She'd watched how Julie had to strap herself onto the ladder and figured she could do that with Hunter...but she had to have his help. She couldn't carry him.

She frantically shook him. "Get up, Hunter, get up!" After a few more times of her yelling at him, he finally stirred, groggily.

Fiona continued to try to get him up and moving. "Hunter, we have to get to the chopper. I need your help." She appealed to the soldier in him, in the side that saved people for a living. "Please, help me get to the ladder," Fiona begged, hoping the desperation she could hear in her own words would break through to him.

It did. Hunter staggered to his feet, with Fiona's help, and with her arm around his waist, he stumbled along beside her to the dangling ladder. Fiona tried to steady Hunter with one hand, while randomly firing his pistol with the other. She knew she wasn't hitting a damn thing, but she hoped the bullets flying would maybe make the bad guys think twice about coming out of hiding. Hunter's teammates in the helicopter were frantically shooting around them, trying to suppress the gunfire from the drug runners as well. Fiona hoped they were as good a shot as she'd always heard. She'd hate to end up dead from a stray bullet after everything she'd been through.

After what seemed like forever, but was really probably only about ten seconds, they reached the ladder. "Help me, Hunter," Fiona fake-begged him again. "Hold on to the ladder to keep it steady for me."

Fiona was completely lying to him, trying to get him

near enough to the first rung so she could strap him in. "Step up, Hunter." She watched him blindly step up to the first rung. Fiona wrapped the containment rope around his back and clipped it to the ladder again. It wasn't much, and probably wouldn't hold him if he passed out on his way up, so she prayed he'd be able to hold on for the short trip up.

"Hold on," Fiona begged Hunter desperately. "For me, hold on. Don't let go." Hunter seemed to become a bit more lucid at her words, and just as his partners were hauling him up, he tried to grab her hand.

Fiona stepped back out of the way and ran back toward the break in the trees where they'd been hiding. She heard him swearing as he was lifted up toward the helicopter.

"Thank God," Fiona sobbed while still trying to randomly shoot his pistol. When she shot the last bullet, she just watched as Hunter miraculously reached the chopper and was hauled inside by several grasping hands. The drug runners were finally backing off as a result of the fire power from the chopper.

Fiona wasn't sure what the men in the helicopter would do. She knew they weren't expecting to pick up more than two people. She didn't even know if they had room for her. But they had to have seen her helping Hunter onto the ladder. Had to have seen she wasn't the enemy. Fiona wanted to see the ladder drop back to the ground for her almost more than she wanted a three course meal, but she had no idea how much weight the chopper could hold and if it was even feasible for Hunter's teammates to save her too.

Fiona grabbed Hunter's pack with the intention of slinging it over her back as she'd seen him do time after time, and almost fell backwards when she tried to pick it up. The thing was heavy! She had no idea how Hunter had been able to carry it as far as he did without seeming to be bothered by it. Fiona wanted to leave it on the ground where Hunter had left it, she honestly didn't feel strong enough to take it with her, but she knew she couldn't leave it behind. Fiona figured there was probably a lot of electronic equipment in it and probably other top secret things.

The other reason she didn't want to leave it behind was because she didn't know if there was any identifying information in it or not, and she didn't want anything coming back to Hunter. She had no time to search it to make sure and the last thing she wanted was some drug dealer in Mexico knowing who Hunter was and possibly coming after him in the States. She had no idea how likely that was, but then again she never would've thought she would've been kidnapped and taken away to be sold into the sex slave trade either.

Fiona laid the pack on the ground and lay down on her back on top of it. She snaked her arms through the straps and struggled to get upright. She put her feet to the side and shifted around. She got her legs under her and used a nearby tree to pull herself painfully to her feet. She fell back once, and luckily there was a tree there to stop her from falling on her ass. Fiona shifted her weight until she felt comfortable standing with the heavy backpack on.

Fiona looked nervously back up at the chopper hovering overhead. It was time for the million dollar question. Would they leave her behind? They'd rescued their man and the original hostage. They'd completed their mission. Would they rescue her too? Or was she too much of an unknown?

Fiona held her breath. If they left, okay, she couldn't think about that, but maybe just maybe…the seconds ticked by. Just as Fiona thought the chopper was going to take off and leave her to fend for herself in the jungle, the ladder started lowering again. Thank God! Fiona almost sobbed in relief, realizing what a close call she'd had. That ladder was literally the difference between life and death for her. Fiona choked back a sob, now wasn't the time or the place to break down. She still had to make it up to, and in, the helicopter alive.

Chapter Seven

FIONA STAGGERED TOWARD the ladder swinging crazily in the air flying around by the blades of the chopper. She couldn't walk in a straight line because of the pack on her back. She was also still trying to shoot randomly into the trees, but she was almost out of ammo. Fiona figured she looked ridiculous, but all she cared about was getting the hell out of the jungle.

She looked up. There were men hanging out of the open door still firing their weapons at the drug runners, but Fiona heard it all through a daze.

Only a little more, Fiona told herself, trying to make herself as small a target as possible, which was really laughable since she had a giant backpack on and was quite tall.

Finally Fiona grabbed the ladder, reaching it just as she started to fall on her face. She stepped up to the first rung, and hung on tight. There was no way she could get the strap around herself with the pack on, so she simply wrapped her arms around the sides of the ladder, buried her head, and hoped like hell Hunter's team-mates would pull her up fast. They did.

Fiona heard a bullet hit the pack on her back and she thought she felt something hit her leg, but amazingly it didn't hurt. She was numb to everything. Her body was shaking from the adrenaline rush like it was twenty degrees outside rather than ninety. Fiona didn't think she'd feel it if a bullet had hit her in the head at that point.

Fiona opened her eyes to check on her progress in getting to the chopper and saw they were flying away from the clearing at a high rate of speed. Terrified she inhaled sharply and squeezed her eyes closed and prayed she'd make it to the chopper quickly.

After what seemed like an eternity, Fiona felt hands on her arms lifting her, practically throwing her into the interior of the helicopter. Her eyes immediately searched for Hunter. He was lying toward the back of the small space with a man dressed all in camouflage giving him first aid.

Fiona looked around for Julie, she also seemed to be fine. She was sitting off to the side with her head buried in the chest of another camo-wearing man.

The two men who'd hauled her aboard the chopper, pantomimed for her to crawl over to the side of the aircraft next to the man who was comforting Julie. Fiona gestured at her back, knowing there was no way she could move with Hunter's pack on her back. One of the men helped her remove the backpack as if she carried feathers instead of what had to be at least a hundred pounds of gear, and she made her way over to where they'd pointed.

It was too loud to talk, and no one would be able to hear her if she did try to speak anyway. Fiona saw the men all wore ear pieces, so she figured they could communicate with each other, even with the noise. She saw their lips moving, but couldn't hear anything but the motor of the helicopter. Fiona didn't care. She was out of the damn jungle and everyone seemed to be okay. At the moment that was all she could muster up inside to care about.

She watched as Hunter's shoulder was bandaged up by one of his teammates. He was unconscious, but at least they'd seemed to stop the bleeding. Fiona realized, with a start, that she'd never been so scared in her life as she was when she saw Hunter fall and the blood seep from him. Even when she'd been grabbed and had woken up to…yeah, even then. Watching Hunter fall after being shot, was scarier than even that. Fiona couldn't say why, it just was.

The chopper flew on and on and after what seemed like forever, finally landed at a dirt covered airstrip. Fiona saw a small plane and figured that was how they were leaving. Just as Fiona got the nerve up to ask about what was going on, Julie was there to ask the questions so Fiona didn't have to.

"Where are we going?" she asked nastily. "I thought we were getting out of here. Why are we stopping? Where's my dad's plane?"

The man who Julie had been clinging to, responded, "Don't worry, Julie, you'll be home soon. Your dad will be glad to see you."

And with that Julie started crying dramatically again.

Fiona turned away. She caught the eye of one of other men. She had to ask, "How will we get back in the United States without passports?" She didn't mean to be the buzz kill of the moment when they were about to get out of the country, but she'd always been too practical. Fiona had asked the question generally. She figured they probably had *Julie's* passport since they were expecting to rescue her, but they didn't even know who she was. How would *Fiona* get back into the country? They wouldn't leave her at the airport would they? She had no idea how these things worked and wished Hunter was awake. Fiona knew he'd explain everything to her and make her feel better.

"Well, we're not going back into the country the usual way." The man chuckled when he answered.

At Fiona's stricken look, he rushed on to reassure her, "Don't worry, all will be fine."

Fiona shut up. Whatever. She was glad that someone else was handling things; she didn't think she could stay upright much longer, nonetheless think about what to do next. The adrenaline was wearing off and Fiona was feeling sick again. She felt like crap, her leg hurt, she stunk to high heaven, and she couldn't get her hands to stop shaking. But she was alive. Hunter was alive. That should be all she cared about at the moment.

They all transferred to a small plane. Hunter was laid down in the back of the plane on a small cot, while Julie and the guy she wouldn't let go of, sat near the front. Two of the men climbed into the cockpit area while the two others got Hunter settled and chose a seat themselves.

Fiona climbed aboard the plane and looked around to decide where she should sit. She didn't want to sit near Julie, she was sure the feeling was mutual, and she didn't want to sit far from Hunter, so she could make sure he was okay. But she didn't want to sit near any of the other men because she knew she was disgusting. She stunk and was covered in filth. Fiona was also uncomfortable with the SEAL's obvious maleness as well. They oozed testosterone out of every pore and now that Fiona was out of the jungle and immediate danger, she couldn't help but remember what other men had done to her while she'd been in captivity.

Fiona also knew another bout with her withdrawal

symptoms was coming. She couldn't control the shaking of her body, just like before. Her leg also hurt, but Hunter needed attention more than she did. She kept quiet. She'd take care of it later.

The trip to wherever they were going, took about three hours. Hunter woke up once and Fiona heard him talking to the men sitting near him. She couldn't hear what they said, but she was so far gone inside her head at that point, that it wouldn't have mattered anyway.

Fiona couldn't stop the shakes and she'd been dry heaving into the air sick bag in the seat pocket in front of her for the last hour. She knew the men thought she was airsick, and that was all right with her. She prayed Hunter wouldn't tell them anything about the drugs. Fiona was embarrassed enough as it was. If she could only get to a hotel, or somewhere, and be left alone, she'd deal with it. Eventually the symptoms had to stop. She just had to wait them out.

Cookie had woken up in the back of the plane. He tried to sit up and was restrained by Wolf and Dude.

"Settle down, Cookie, you're okay," Wolf told him in a low calm voice.

Cookie hurt like hell, but there was something he had to do, something he had to remember.

Wolf saw his confusion and tried to reassure him. "The women are safe, don't worry. You got them out. Not sure who the second broad is, but they're both okay. Only you could pick up a woman in the jungle, Cookie!"

That was it! Cookie caught Dude's arm as he leaned over him to check his shoulder wound. Wolf also leaned toward his teammate to hear what he had to say.

Looking at each of his teammates, Cookie urgently said, "Fee. Help her, don't let her go." It was all he got out before he passed out again.

Dude tucked Cookie's arm back by his side and he and Wolf looked at each other, realizing that Cookie cared for the second woman. Neither knew what had happened in the jungle, but he'd specifically been worried about the woman he'd called Fee, not Julie.

Even though Cookie couldn't hear him, Dude told him softly, "Don't worry, Cookie, we'll take care of her for you until you can see to her yourself."

The plane landed with a bump and a slide. Fiona took a deep breath. This was it. It was time to get on with her life. She didn't know where they were, but she'd figure it out. She always figured it out.

Julie and one of the men got out of the plane first, then the two pilots, then her, then Hunter was carried out by the two men who'd been seeing to him. Fiona knew the men were Hunter's team. She'd recognized their names from when Hunter had told them to her what seemed like ages ago.

One of the men who'd been in the back with

Hunter had been called Wolf by one of the other men. She was so glad Hunter was with his team. They'd take care of him.

Fiona squinted as they emerged out of the plane and into the sunshine. They were on another deserted dirt airstrip, but this time there was a van waiting for them. It was hot, but the sun felt wonderful on her face. Fiona hadn't seen the sun directly in months. Besides, she was freezing. She knew she shouldn't have been, but she was. Fiona staggered and Wolf was there to catch her arm.

"You okay?" he asked.

Fiona didn't like the scrutiny the big man was giving her so she simply nodded and moved away. She just wanted to be alone.

All eight of them climbed in a van and the same two men who'd been helping Hunter before, arranged him across one of the seats and climbed in behind him. Fiona managed to crawl in without assistance, and watched as Julie and the others also settled themselves into their seats. It was all done without a word spoken. Even Julie wasn't babbling now. It was weird, but Fiona didn't have time to even care. She wasn't in Mexico anymore. That was all she cared about at the moment. They headed down the road and away from the little plane.

It didn't matter where they were going, just that they were going somewhere away from the jungle. Her feet hurt like a bitch, so hopefully they didn't have to walk far. Looking down at them, Fiona had no idea how she was going to get her damn flip-flops off. Hunter had taped the hell out of them in an effort to protect her.

They drove for a while until they reached a crappy little house in the middle of nowhere. Another van was waiting. They repeated the drill from before, and everyone got settled. The men had put Hunter in the back of the van this time and he was sprawled on the back seat. Wolf was sitting near him making sure all was well. Fiona hoped they were bringing him to a hospital. She didn't like to see him so quiet and still.

Finally, after driving for another fifteen minutes or so, Fiona started to see signs of civilization. A few houses here and there, then finally some stores. Eventually, they pulled up to another small airport, this one with an actual concrete runway spread out behind the small building. Fiona didn't have any identification so she had no idea how she'd be able to fly commercially, but again, she kept quiet and waited for the SEALs to tell her what was going on and what she should do.

When the van stopped, Fiona watched as the men all got out, except for Wolf, who was monitoring Hunter. No one motioned for her to stay, so Fiona climbed out too, but stayed close to the van...and Hunter. She knew eventually she'd have to leave him, but if they weren't going to ask her to do it right now, she wouldn't. Just being near him comforted her. She knew it was because he'd rescued her, but she also thought it was more. What more, she couldn't say…just more.

Fiona saw a limo pull up nearby. An older man got out of the limo and it finally clicked. This must be Julie's father. It was. Julie shrieked and threw herself toward the man and hugged him close. She saw the man close his eyes and embrace his daughter. As annoying as Julie was, Fiona couldn't help but tear up. If it wasn't for his man and his daughter she'd still be in that hellhole with no hope of rescue.

She stayed glued to the side of the van watching the drama unfold in front of her. A part of her wanted to thank the man herself, but she just wasn't feeling up to it. She'd have to step away from the van, walk across the space separating the van and limo, explain who she was and…Fiona stopped thinking. It just wasn't worth it.

Fiona watched as one of the men who'd rescued them, approached the Senator and Julie. The Senator had a short conversation with the military man, without letting go of his daughter, then they shook hands, nodded at each other, and that was that. The man led Julie away. They got into the limo and the door closed behind them.

Fiona sighed. She hadn't liked the woman, but it was almost anticlimactic to see her just walk away without a backward glance. Fiona shivered, put Julie out of her mind, and turned to watch the men as they headed back toward her to the van. She had no idea what would happen next. She didn't have long to wait to find out.

"Hop back in, Fiona," Wolf called from inside the van. He held out his hand to help her back inside.

"But…" Fiona said, looking between the airport and Wolf sitting in the vehicle. She shrugged. She obviously wasn't going to be flying anywhere, not looking or smelling like she did, and certainly not without any identification.

She climbed back in without Wolf's help. When the van was on its way again, Fiona finally asked, "Are we taking him to the hospital?" gesturing toward Hunter.

No one answered her at first. Finally one of the other men in the van said, "No, we have our own medical facility nearby. It doesn't behoove us to show up at the local hospital looking like we do sometimes. Don't worry; we'll take good care of him."

Fiona nodded like it made perfect sense, not knowing her furrowed brow gave away her confusion. Nothing made sense. They hadn't asked who she was, they hadn't asked where she came from, hadn't commented on the way she looked or smelled, they hadn't really asked her anything. Just took it for granted that she was there. It confused the hell out of Fiona, and that wasn't a good feeling, on top of everything else. Was she safe with them? What if they dumped her somewhere?

Just as she started to freak out, Wolf said, "Stop fretting, Fiona."

At the use of her name for the second time, Fiona started.

Wolf noticed, and tried to reassure her. "Cookie told us who you were when we hauled him in the chopper, well at least your name. He was cursing a blue-streak saying you disobeyed him. We thought he was hallucinating until he told us your name when he woke up briefly in the plane."

They all laughed and Fiona looked down at her lap. Fiona knew Hunter would be mad that she deceived him to get him on the helicopter, but honestly, it'd been for his own good.

Wolf continued seriously, "He also asked us to look after you until he got better. But it honestly doesn't matter who you are or where you came from, Fiona, you saved his life. That makes you one of us. And we take care of our own. We'll figure out the other stuff in due time, but in the meantime, we'll take of him and we'll take care of you."

Fiona just stared at Wolf. "What?" she asked dumbly. She couldn't get her brain to work right. She was tired, scared, sick, and hurting.

"Just relax," Wolf soothed, seeing how stressed out

she was. "We won't hurt you and you'll soon get to rest. I know you're confused and hungry and tired, and probably scared as well. Let me introduce you to everyone, that might help make you feel better. Okay?"

Fiona nodded. What else could she do?

"I'm Wolf. Up there driving is Benny. Dude and Mozart are sitting in the seat in front of you, and that's Abe next to you. I think you probably know we're all on the same Navy SEAL team. I meant what I said. You saved Cookie's life. You're a part of us now too."

Fiona meekly nodded her head. She had no clue what the hell Wolf was talking about. She felt as if she was in an alternative world. She wasn't one of them. She didn't even *know* them. Whatever. As long as they'd take care of Hunter she didn't care what they said. Fiona just wished they'd hurry up and get to wherever it was they were going. She wanted to… no, she *needed* to lie down.

Chapter Eight

THE VAN FINALLY pulled up to a gate, Benny punched in a code and drove through with the gate closing behind him. Fiona watched it close warily. Was this another form of prison for her? She didn't want to believe it, but the drug withdrawal was taking its toll. She felt nervous and jittery and couldn't trust her own judgment. Fiona's head was spinning and she felt paranoid. Dear God, she needed to be alone.

Fiona stepped out of the van as soon as she could after it came to a stop. She looked up at a beautiful house. It was a huge two story building with windows all around the upper floor. There was an old fashioned porch attached to the front with three rocking chairs. The front door was painted a dark red and she could see red curtains around the windows on the first floor. She had no idea whose house it was. It looked perfectly harmless, but for some reason it made Fiona nervous as hell.

Fiona watched as the men got out of the van and

Wolf and Dude took Hunter into the house through the front door. Fiona took one more look around the yard, noticing the manicured lawn and bushes and slowly hobbled in behind the rest of the men. Before Wolf went down the hall behind Hunter, he took Fiona's arm and led her toward a door.

"Fiona, this is your room. It has a bathroom attached. Please take your time and get changed and clean. I'll bring some scissors down in a bit to help you get those shoes off your feet if you need it. I'll also find some clothes for you to put on after your shower. They'll probably be too big, but they'll be clean. We'll eat once you're ready." Wolf opened the door and watched Fiona walk in the room; he smiled at her then closed the door.

Holy hell, Fiona didn't know what was going on. She'd gone from living in her own filth and peeing in a bucket, to standing in the most beautiful room she'd ever seen. It was absolutely gorgeous. It was huge and the carpet was a pristine white. Fiona didn't want to walk across it to the shower. She knew she'd get it dirty. What had Wolf been thinking leaving her here?

Fiona finally staggered toward the bathroom, ignoring the dirt she knew she was tracking through the room. She entered, then closed the door carefully and locked it firmly behind her. The bathroom was as beautiful as the rest of the room. There were two sinks and a huge marble counter. There was a Jacuzzi tub and a separate shower that had at least three shower heads.

Fiona would have admired it more carefully, but she was at the end of her rope. She'd simply been through too much, and her body wasn't able to support her anymore. She sunk to the floor next to the sink, having the presence of mind to push the plush white rug out of the way, and toppled over. The last thing Fiona thought was with as bad as she felt, she hoped she would die.

COOKIE FINALLY REGAINED consciousness. Wolf had sat next to him for thirty minutes, making sure the IV was opened all the way and that the wound in his shoulder was closed up properly. Mozart had done the honors for that. Wolf knew he was the best one of them to do it. Mozart had sewn up Wolf's Caroline when she'd been hurt. Wolf could barely see the scar on Caroline's side anymore. Mozart was that good.

The bullet had luckily gone all the way through Cookie's shoulder, so Mozart didn't have to dig it out. With luck, it hadn't hit any major arteries, but had put two holes in Cookie's arm. He was on some serious pain killers, but Cookie was a SEAL through and through. He was able to be functional, even with the drugs coursing through his body, especially since he was worried about Fiona.

"Tell me what happened," Cookie demanded of his friend and teammate. "I remember Julie going up to the chopper and then only snippets after that. Fee did get in right?"

Wolf nodded. "The short version is that you were shot, Fiona half dragged you to the ladder and strapped you in, we hauled you up while she went back and got your pack. She shot at the tangos while we re-lowered the ladder. She staggered to it loaded down with your pack; we hauled her up while relocating away from there. We changed to a plane, landed here in Texas, sent Julie off on her way, and now we're here in the safehouse Tex arranged for us. Now...you tell *me* what the hell happened out there."

Cookie knew what Wolf meant. They hadn't suspected a second hostage. Cookie told Wolf as much as he knew, which wasn't much. He didn't want to tell him too much about Fiona's condition yet, as he knew it embarrassed her. But he knew eventually his teammates would have to know. They couldn't help her with the drug withdrawal if they didn't know about it. Cookie wanted to know more about Fiona and where she came from and how she'd ended up in that hellhole he'd found her in before he spoke with Wolf.

The door to Cookie's room popped open and Benny stuck his head in.

"I brought the scissors and change of clothes to Fiona's room, and when she didn't answer the door, I looked in. She was in the bathroom and when I knocked on that door to let her know I'd brought her some things, no one answered. I knocked harder and she still didn't answer. She's not in the shower and I'm worried."

Cookie immediately started to get up at hearing Benny's words. If Benny was worried, Cookie was fucking terrified. Wolf stopped him. "I've got it," he told his injured teammate, but Cookie wasn't listening.

"Help me up," he told Wolf gruffly. All he knew was he wasn't going to lie around if Fiona was hurt. Wolf didn't object, just sighed and helped Cookie to his feet and toward Fiona's room.

Abe was at Fiona's bathroom door when the other men arrived. "We didn't want to barge in on her if she was in the tub," Abe explained further, "but we can't get her to open the door. She says she's okay, but she doesn't sound good."

Wolf knocked on the door again and when there was no answer, helped Cookie get closer. Wolf gestured at him to take a shot at getting through to her.

"Fiona?" Cookie called out, "Can you hear me? Open the door, sweetheart." The endearment came out without conscious thought.

Fiona couldn't stop shaking. Her body was rebelling against her. She couldn't breathe that well, and she knew something was seriously wrong. She thought she heard Hunter's voice, but that couldn't be right. He was unconscious…wasn't he?

Cookie tried again, his voice a bit more forceful than before. "Fee, open the door right now or we're coming in." He paused. "I'm worried about you. Come on, open the door so I can see you're all right."

Fiona roused herself again. It *was* him. "Hunter?" she said weakly. "Are you okay?" She heard him laugh.

"Hell, Fee, I'm fine, it's *you* we're worried about. Now, open the door." He said the last a bit more harshly then he intended to.

"I can't come to the door right now, Hunter," Fiona tried to explain, not really knowing what she was saying. "Maybe later." She put her head back on the cold tile floor and closed her eyes.

Cookie gestured toward Benny. He was the best lock picker they had. They could all open just about any door and any lock, but Benny was the master at it. He could always manage to open any lock much faster than the rest of them. And this was certainly a situation where time was of the essence. Benny had the door open within a few seconds. The door swung wide and Cookie's stomach dropped to the floor.

Wolf was at Fiona's side before Cookie could move. She lay motionless on the bathroom tile, just as filthy as the last time Cookie had seen her. She'd managed to get into the bathroom, but not to clean herself up in any way. It was if she'd entered the room and fell to the ground immediately. Wolf easily lifted Fiona's unconscious body and headed back toward the medical rooms with Cookie at his back following closely.

Wolf laid Fiona down carefully on the bed Cookie had just gotten out of, and looked back at Benny and Abe. "I need warm water. Lots of it. We have to get her clean before we do anything else. Grab the scissors too so we can get those shoes off her feet."

Cookie looked on helplessly. He was feeling weak and swayed on his feet.

Wolf paused in his care of Fiona to drag a chair over toward the bed she was lying on and forced Cookie into it. "Sit, Cookie," he told him sternly, "before you fall down, you stubborn ass."

Abe and Benny came back with the water, towels, and scissors. They all started wiping down Fiona's limbs, trying to get as much dirt and crud off her as they could without a full-fledged bath or shower. They moved quickly and professionally. Fiona moaned, but didn't protest in any way.

Benny started with her feet. He cut the tape off and peeled the flip-flops off her feet. Her feet were absolutely filthy. He could see Fiona had blisters on the tops of her feet where the rubber of the shoes had rubbed against her skin. The amount of dirt and crud on the bottom of her feet was almost hard to believe. Benny dropped the shoes on the ground and carefully pulled off her shorts. He wasn't even paying attention to how she looked; he was one hundred percent concentrating on getting this woman somewhat clean so they could give her any other medical aid she'd need.

Cookie watched absently as his teammates cleaned Fiona. He wasn't upset that they were touching her and that Benny had removed her pants, he was too worried about why Fiona was unconscious and what was wrong with her.

Abe and Wolf cut Cookie's long sleeved black shirt off of Fiona, which wasn't hard to do since it was so large on her. They swore at the first glimpse they had of the metal collar around her neck. The shirt had hidden it until now.

"Jesus," Cookie heard Abe mutter under his breath. They could all see how red her neck was. The rusted metal had rubbed her skin raw. It'd probably already been sore before they'd escaped, but now, after their mad dash through the jungle, it was beyond sore. It was red and inflamed and the amount of dried blood around it was somewhat alarming.

Abe continued removing her shirt, pulling it out from under her. Throughout it all, Cookie kept his eyes on Fiona's face. She hadn't moved, she hadn't moaned, she hadn't cried. She just lay on the bed, completely out of it.

The men continued their cleaning. They had warm washcloths they were using to try to get the worst of the dirt and grime off of Fiona. With each swipe, the washcloths were becoming more and more dirty, the water they'd been rinsing the rags in was practically black with the filth that was coming off her body.

Suddenly, at the same time Benny said, "Hell," Wolf said, "Shit."

Cookie looked away from Fiona's face for the first time, wondering what they'd found. He'd clearly heard the grimness in each of his friends' tones.

Benny gestured toward her leg. They all saw what they'd missed before. The dirt and grime had hidden a bullet wound. It looked like just a graze, but it was now slowly oozing blood over her leg and onto the sheet. The washcloth had obviously removed the scab that had been forming and allowed it to start bleeding again.

Both men looked at Abe, wondering what he'd been alarmed about. He simply gestured to her arms. The inside of Fiona's elbows were covered in needle marks and bruises. Cookie had seen them before, but it'd obviously come as a surprise to the other men.

No one questioned Cookie, no one looked disgusted. They just continued to work in silence to try to wipe away this courageous woman's time in hell. And it'd obviously been a hellacious experience. Besides the track marks and filthy condition of her body, bruises were revealed as the dirt was wiped away. She had different colors of finger marks on her upper arms, and more alarming, on her waist. There was a boot sized fading bruise on her back, but the most alarming were the bruises on her inner thighs, all different colors, alerting the men to the fact that some were older than others.

The track marks on her arms were ugly, but it really didn't matter in the long run. Even if Fiona had taken the drugs eagerly, which none of them would blame her for; this woman had saved their teammate's life. She'd saved their *friend's* life. They all had questions, but they'd wait. Her health came first.

All went well until Wolf tried to put an IV into Fiona's arm. One second she was deadweight in their arms, allowing them to move her limbs wherever they needed to in order to get her undressed and clean, and the next she fighting them as if her life depended on it.

"No no no *no*," Fiona screamed out, fighting with all she had. She kicked out with her feet and narrowly missed Abe, who was standing near her. She was obviously remembering how she'd been drugged, or worse, been violated.

"Get off me, assholes," Fiona snarled, while still twisting and turning in the men's grasps. Fiona almost managed to twist off the bed and onto the floor before Wolf and Benny got a hold of her limbs and held her down, which only made her fight more frantically.

Cookie quickly leaned down toward Fiona's head. "Fiona, snap out of it," he said harshly, trying to get through to her. He put his hand from his good arm on her forehead. She stilled. Cookie continued, leaning in until his lips were right at her ear. "It's me, Hunter. You're safe. You're back in the States; you aren't in that shack anymore. Do you hear me?"

Fiona didn't respond, but she didn't fight either.

"I'm here with you and you're in the hospital with me. We aren't drugging you. I swear on my life you're safe. Do you hear me? We're trying to put in an IV. It'll give you fluids; it'll make you feel better. We aren't drugging you. I promise."

Still no movement from Fiona. "Trust me, sweetheart," Cookie tried again. "Please, just trust me."

Fiona finally sighed and turned toward Hunter. Her eyes opened into slits, just enough to see. "Hunter?" she said tentatively. "You're really okay?"

"I'm really okay," Cookie was touched in a way he'd never been before at her unselfishness. She had to be hurting and was confused, and still, she was worried about him. Cookie moved his hand from her forehead to the side of her face. Her skin was hot and sweaty, but Cookie could feel her lean her head into his hand as he spoke. The thought that in the midst of her terror, she'd trust him, made his stomach clench with an unfamiliar, but not unwelcome, jolt. "Just relax, Fee, everything is fine. I'm here and I'm not going anywhere."

Fiona sighed and nodded. Her eyes went to Wolf and the other men and unknowingly impressed the hell out of the battle-hardened men standing around her. "Sorry guys, I'll try to stay still, can't promise though."

Abe was the first one to respond, and he did so chuckling under his breath. "No worries, Fiona. We'll take care of you. *Nothing* will hurt you here. Relax."

Wolf was able to put in the IV without further incident, but all four men watched as she scrunched her eyes closed and as the sweat popped out on her forehead. Fiona finally fell into a fevered sleep without another word.

Wolf turned toward Cookie with barely leashed anger toward the mystery men who'd drugged and abused Fiona in his eyes, and said between clenched teeth, "Spill it." They all needed to hear Fiona's story. This obviously wasn't a cut-and-dried case. They all needed to hear what was going on, and it'd have to be reported back to their commander.

Cookie sighed. "I'd hoped she was over the worst of it, but apparently I was wrong. They drugged her. I have no idea with what, but I'm assuming it was probably heroin, but her symptoms don't exactly fit. Heroin withdrawal usually includes things like agitation, muscle aches, nausea, and vomiting. She's experienced all of those, but they usually don't last much longer than thirty hours. She should be over that by now.

"But if they mixed the heroin with meth, that could definitely cause some sort of substance-induced psychotic disorder. That makes this withdrawal more serious. It has its own set of symptoms, the prominent one being delusions or hallucinations. Fiona said they'd been drugging her for weeks. She's embarrassed about it, and you can see she's fighting as hard as she can, but it's not enough. I'm afraid it's going to get bad. I'm amazed she made it as long as she did."

"She's obviously tough," Wolf told Cookie. "She'll handle this. We won't let her down."

Wolf had apparently adopted Fiona as one of their own. He'd watched her put her life on the line for one of his best friends. There was no way one of the team could've safely gone down from the helicopter to help out and to get Cookie up. Fiona had literally saved both of their lives.

"We have to figure out what we're going to do. We can't stay here forever. Tex's people are only allowing us to use this place for about a week and a half at most, and we have to report back to base. I'll call the commander and let him know what's up and that all of us won't be returning right away. We have to figure out who's staying to help take care of her and who's going."

"I'm not leaving her, Wolf," Cookie said with steel in his voice.

"I didn't think you were." It was said matter-of-factly, as if Wolf hadn't even thought of the possibility.

"I'll stay too," Benny told them. Before Abe could volunteer to stay as well, Benny continued. "Abe, you need to get home to Alabama. You know how much she stresses when you're gone. Wolf, you should probably get home too, you can talk to the commander and make sure you hold the fort down, besides, Caroline will be just as anxious to see you as Alabama is to see Abe. I'll get Dude to stay here with us."

"What about Mozart?" Abe asked, apparently having no issues with Benny's plan.

"I think he can probably go back home as well. If we need him though, we'll get in touch. We can play it by ear."

"Cookie? Does that sound all right to you?" Wolf wanted to make sure Cookie approved whatever they decided, this woman was obviously important to him, even though they'd just met. Wolf didn't question it. He'd made a connection with his Caroline just as quickly and if Cookie was feeling half of what he'd felt when he'd found out Caroline was injured, he knew Fiona was already a part of their close-knit SEAL family, even if she didn't know it yet.

Cookie ran his hand over Fiona's forehead, feeling the heat and dampness. He moved slowly and carefully, still feeling the pain of his own wound. "Yeah, I'll get her through this and we'll see where we stand." His voice lowered in pain. "I don't really know anything about her. I don't know if she has a family somewhere wondering where she is. If she's married, if she has kids…" his voice trailed off.

The mood in the room got heavy. Christ, they hadn't thought of that. Wolf cleared his throat. "The main thing is to get her well. Cookie, you can deal with all that after she recovers."

Cookie nodded. "Okay, you guys get going. Benny and Dude can stay here with me. Wolf, if you can talk to Tex and let him know we'll be holed up here for a bit longer I'd appreciate it. I'll stay in touch and let you know how Fiona is doing and what our next steps will be."

The other men left the room, each looking back one more time at the woman on the bed and their team-mate. They all silently hoped she'd pull through and that she was free. It was plain to see Cookie already considered Fiona "his," and they hoped, for both their sakes, it could work out.

Chapter Nine

FIONA'S FEVER SPIKED. Cookie was in the room with her when she started thrashing on the bed. She was extremely hot to the touch. Cookie grabbed Fiona's hand to try to reassure her, but that only seemed to make her reaction worse, and it pushed her over the edge. She jerked away from him and sat up, obviously trying to get up and out of the bed.

"Duuuude," Cookie bellowed as he tried to hold Fiona still. He wasn't very effective with his own shoulder injured from being shot. The door slammed open and not only Dude, but Benny also entered the room and summed up the situation quickly.

Dude grabbed hold of Fiona's shoulders while Benny grabbed her shins. Cookie stayed at her head trying to calm Fiona down with his touch. All three men were silent while they watched Fiona twist and turn and struggle to release herself. Just as before, her efforts only exhausted her. This time when Cookie tried to gentle her with his voice, it did no good. His voice couldn't bring her out of the drug induced haze she was in this time.

Finally, after what seemed hours, but was really only ten minutes or so, Fiona fell still again. She opened her eyes, gazing duly around the room. With glazed eyes she whimpered, "Why? Why are you doing this to me?" and then fell silent once again.

"God damn," Benny exclaimed softly. "Let us know when she wakes up again," he told Cookie sadly, knowing it probably wouldn't be the last time they were needed. "We're just next door and can be here in a second."

"I will, thanks guys. Hopefully she'll sleep the worst of this off soon."

Nodding, Benny and Dude left Cookie alone with Fiona again.

Cookie slept fitfully for the next twenty four hours. Waking when Fiona woke, trying to soothe her, calling for Benny and Dude to help him keep Fiona from hurting herself when needed, and then trying to sleep when Fiona slept.

They'd actually had to put gloves on Fiona's hands because she kept trying to scratch her skin. He knew it probably felt like her skin was crawling with bugs, but it was just the withdrawal making her think that way…okay, and the multitude of bug bites as well.

Cookie had seen a lot of hard things in his life, but

nothing had prepared him for the heartbreaking cries and pleading that came out of this woman's mouth. They were all the more horrifying because he knew if *she* knew she was doing it, she'd have been mortified. Fiona had done everything she could while they were in the jungle to downplay her own suffering, and there was no doubt she'd been suffering.

When Fiona was lucid enough, they all tried to get her to eat something. They knew she wasn't dehydrated because the IVs were pumping lots of life saving fluids into her nonstop, but they were worried about her caloric intake.

They frequently got her up and she was able to use the toilet. Cookie was relieved because he knew Fiona *definitely* wouldn't want them putting in a catheter. They were all amazed she was as mobile as she was. Cookie attributed that to her stubbornness and strong will. She still wasn't lucid, but they all hoped she'd soon come out on the other side of the worst of this soon.

Three days after they arrived, Fiona opened her eyes and watched Cookie sitting next to her in a chair by the bed. She didn't say anything, but waited for him to open his eyes. As if Cookie could feel her gaze on him, he stirred and his eyes came to hers as soon as he awakened.

"How do you feel today, Fiona?" Cookie asked warily, wondering what kind of mood she'd be in and how the withdrawal was affecting her today. He'd seen Fiona's eyes open before, and she'd been completely out of it, not knowing what she was saying or doing. Cookie hoped today was the day she'd break through and come back to him.

Fiona cleared her throat before she spoke. "Better."

Cookie nodded, and kept a watchful eye on her. She sounded awful, but he wasn't surprised with all she'd been through. "Do you feel like getting up to use the bathroom?"

Fiona blushed and nodded.

Cookie was thrilled to see the blush bloom across Fiona's face. In the past couple of days she'd acted like a zombie, and certainly hadn't reacted with embarrassment to anything she'd done, or that the guys had done to her. Cookie helped Fiona stand up and arranged her IV pole and walked her to the bathroom. When he went to go in with her, Fiona stopped him.

"I can do it," she told him sternly, not looking Cookie in the eyes.

Cookie was skeptical, but didn't want to hurt Fiona's feelings. "Okay, if you need my help, just say something, I'll be right here," and he gestured at the door. Fiona nodded and closed the door softly.

Cookie heard her engage the lock on the door and frowned. It wasn't as if the lock would keep him or anyone else out, but it was more the fact she felt like she had to lock it at all that bothered him. He waited not-so-patiently for her to finish up so he could put her back to bed.

Fiona didn't bother to look at herself in the mirror, she didn't bother to use the toilet, she immediately went to the small window in the bathroom. She had to get out of here. Who knew what they were planning on doing with her. She knew sometimes they liked to be nice to her to try to get her to let her guard down, then do something horrible to crush her spirits. "Never again," Fiona mumbled to herself. She wanted out. She had to get out.

Her hands were shaking, she felt horrible, but she reached for the window anyway, noticing for the first time as she did, the IV in her arm. Feeling repulsed, who knew what they were putting in her body now, Fiona tore it out, not trying to be gentle or to worry about doing it the "right way." Blood slowly oozed down her arm and dripped on the floor, but she paid no attention to it.

Fiona slowly raised the window and glanced outside. Luckily, it seemed to be night. She had lost all sense of what day it was and when it was. When she was first taken, she'd tried to keep track, but the days and nights soon all ran together. But now the darkness would help her get away. Fiona looked outside again. Unluckily, she wasn't on the first floor...she looked to her right...a drain pipe ran the length of the wall right by the window. It wasn't perfect, but it'd have to work.

Fiona paused momentarily, something was niggling at the back of her brain, something about being on the second floor rather than the first. She ignored it. Time was of the essence. She had to escape. At any time they could notice she was gone. Her only thought was to get out. Get out now. Fiona awkwardly climbed up on the toilet to get better access to the window and lifted one leg. Feeling weak and shaky, she forced her body to cooperate and eased herself out. She reached for the drainpipe and held on.

Benny was sleeping when he felt the silent alarm on his wrist vibrate. Tex had told them the house was completely wired. No one could get in or out undetected. No one had thought they'd really need it while Fiona recuperated, but it was second nature for all of them to be hyper-vigilant.

Surprised, Benny shot out of bed and threw open his bedroom door and tore down the hall into the make-shift control room. The main control-room was actually set up downstairs in a bunker-type compound under the den, but they'd been spending so much time upstairs with Fiona, they'd all agreed to move some aspects of it up here, so it'd be closer, just in case.

Benny took one look at the television monitor and swore. Fuck. Benny whirled and raced down the hall and down the stairs. Without bothering to contact either of his teammates or disable the alarm to the house, figuring it would wake Dude up, just as it did him, Benny ran around the side of the building not knowing exactly what to expect, even after seeing it on the monitors, and looked up. "Aw, hell," he muttered.

Fiona tried to slip slowly down the drainpipe, but her hands were bloody from where she had pulled out the IV and she had no strength. She slid faster and faster toward the ground. All she could do was try to hang on. Benny grabbed Fiona just before she hit the ground. Just as he caught her, Dude came running around the corner of the building, gun drawn, ready for anything.

Fiona felt someone grab her just as she was about to escape. She'd been so close this time. She tried to throw herself out of the arms of the man who held her, but his hold was too tight.

"Let me go, let me *go*," she croaked at him while trying to hit him and scratch his eyes out. Benny grunted and grasped her closer to his chest. Dude summed up the situation quickly, looked up at the window and boomed, "Cooookie."

Cookie heard Dude yelling for him and knew something was very wrong. Yelling wasn't their usual mode of communication, so if Dude was shouting from outside at the top of his lungs, something had seriously gone wrong. He had to get to Fiona and protect her.

With one strong push against the bathroom door with his shoulder, the door slammed open as if the lock had never been engaged. His heart hit the floor. He tried to process the empty room, IV pole standing upright, and the blood splatters covering the wall and the window…and, of course, the *open* window.

Cookie strode over and looked out. "Fucking hell." He saw Benny struggling with Fiona, and Dude kneeling, trying to hold her legs. She was crying and struggling and trying to get out of their arms. A part of him saw the blood covering her arms but tried to block it out. Cookie didn't say a word, but turned around and headed down the stairs to get to Fiona.

When he got outside, Cookie saw that Benny had sat on the ground and was holding Fiona in a wrestler's hold she couldn't escape from. He had one arm diagonally around her chest and the other was locked around her head, keeping her immobile, but allowing her plenty of room to breathe. Dude was kneeling next to them holding Fiona down with his hands on her legs above her knees. Fiona's arms were trapped at her sides within Benny's grasp. She looked up at Cookie with tears and fire in her eyes at the same time.

"Let me go, you fucking bastards. You can't keep me here. Let me go, just let me go."

Benny looked up at Cookie sadly. "Guess she's still not out of the worst of it yet."

Cookie nodded grimly at his teammate's not-needed words, and squatted awkwardly down next to Benny, Dude, and Fiona.

"Fiona, it's Hunter, you're okay, you're fine. You're in Texas." He had to try to get through to her.

"Shut *up*!" she yelled viciously while trying to wriggle out of the inescapable hold of Benny at the same time. "I don't believe you, you're an asshole and I'm gonna kill you, I'm gonna tear your fucking arms off and poke out your eyes, just see if I don't." Fiona tried to spit at him, but her spittle landed a couple inches away from her hip, instead of on Cookie.

"I won't do it, I won't do anything you tell me to do, you hear me? I *won't*. You're sick. You can't *sell* people. We're not *slaves*. Raping people and hurting and drugging them until they do what you want them to is a shitty thing to do." She paused, her breath hitching in her throat, but she continued. "I'll *never* be a 'good little girl' and let someone keep me as their sex slave. *Never*. You hear me? You might as well kill me now. Just do it already. *Fucking do it*!"

Cookie stood up. Angrier than he could remember being in a long time. Not at Fiona, but at her kidnappers. *They* had done this to her. He knew she was reliving some of the hell they'd put her through. Knew Fiona thought they were them. Cookie wanted to get on a plane, head back to Mexico, and hunt them down.

They'd hurt Fiona. They'd done all sorts of unspeakable things to her. To *his* Fiona. He wanted to kill them all. Cookie knew had to get control of himself. While he might want to kill them, he had to take care of Fiona first. She'd always come first now. Always. He had no idea what the future would hold for them, he only knew he wanted to be in it with her.

"You got her?" Cookie asked Benny through clenched teeth. He wanted to be the one holding Fiona, but he knew his strength wasn't at a hundred percent yet, and he didn't want to risk either dropping her or having her escape and hurt herself further.

Benny nodded. Dude helped Benny stand up since he couldn't use his arms because they were holding Fiona. The four of them awkwardly made their way back into the house and up the stairs. Fiona hurled insults and threatened bodily harm to anyone and everyone the entire way.

None of the men said a word as they moved, as one, back up the stairs and toward her room. Not one man was disgusted, not one man pitied her. Every one of them knew Fiona's story now, with the few words she'd spat at them outside, she'd revealed everything she'd been through. They could read between the lines. The curse words and insults she continued to scream at them as they headed upstairs were a result of the drugs and what had happened to her. They all knew it and understood it.

SEAL teams are notoriously close; they have to be as they put their lives in each other's hands on every mission. It's ground into them from the first day of BUD/S training. But this, this was something new. Benny, Dude, and Cookie had never felt as close as they did at this moment. No words were spoken while Fiona was carried back into her bed and restrained. This woman had been through hell, but wasn't broken. Wasn't beaten. She was fighting until her last breath. She was outnumbered and weak, but she still fought. It was humbling and amazing. The three men had seen bravery before. They'd seen Caroline take a beating that would've broken most men. They'd seen her get thrown into the ocean; ankles tied together, and still have the inner strength to stay calm. But somehow, this was something altogether different.

They wanted vengeance for Fiona, something they knew they might never get. But all three men silently vowed to do whatever it took to make sure Fiona felt safe again. Somehow, someway, they'd make her feel safe.

Chapter Ten

FIONA STRUGGLED WEAKLY on the bed. They'd tied her down, again. At least she wasn't chained by the neck anymore. And she wasn't on the hard floor. Again, there was something she should remember...but it was gone as soon as the thought flitted through her brain. They wanted to hurt her, they *had* hurt her. They wanted to sell her. They wanted to kill her.

She watched as one of the men standing next to her filled a syringe. His back was turned, but Fiona knew what he was doing. Oh God. Not again. Not more drugs. Fiona wouldn't beg, she'd done that before and it'd done no good and had only made her feel more pathetic.

"I won't beg, you assholes," Fiona flung out recklessly, looking at the two other men in the room. She blinked to try to clear her vision, but continued, even though she couldn't see them clearly. "You can drug me all you want, but it won't help. I won't do what you say, even if I never get out of here, you'll all pay. I swear to

God. I can't stop you from drugging me, but it won't help you sell me. I'll make sure that anyone you sell me to regrets it and comes to take it out on you."

Fiona's voice trailed off. The roaring in her ears was loud. She could hear her own breathing, but that was it. Oh God, he really was going to drug her again. She closed her eyes and turned her head as far to the side as she could. She couldn't fight anymore. They held her down and she felt the prick of the needle in her arm. Shit. Fiona's thoughts became more and more muddled and she welcomed the nothingness that came over her. She didn't want to know what they'd do to her this time while she was out of it.

The men sighed. Thank God. Thank God the valium Benny had given her had taken effect quickly. No one said a word. Dude got busy putting another IV in her other arm. Cookie tried to clean up the blood on her body. Benny got to work cleaning the bathroom.

Dude was the first one to leave to go back to his bedroom. Benny and Cookie sat on either side of Fiona's bed and watched her. She was breathing a bit fast, but otherwise seemed to be calm.

"Holy shit, Cookie," Benny finally said. Cookie could only nod. They both were imaging the hell Fiona had been through. The fact that she hadn't backed down, that she still wasn't backing down, said a lot about her.

"You know, when I saw you get shot from the chopper, for a moment I wondered what the fuck we were gonna do. We had one hostage rescued, you had an unknown other person with you and you were shot. I almost took her out."

Benny looked away from Fiona's face and at Cookie for the first time since he'd started talking. "We had no idea she was there too, and all I could think of was that she was expendable and you weren't. I had my finger on the trigger and I was ready to fire when I saw her stumble out of that bush with you. She half dragged you, half carried you to that ladder. As soon as I saw you were secure, we hauled your ass up as fast as we could. Even at that point I thought about getting the hell out of there. We still didn't know who she was, and we had both you and the hostage rescued."

Benny paused, then took a deep breath and continued. "I opened my mouth to tell Wolf to get us out of there when I saw her struggling with your pack. Fiona simply looked up at the chopper and waited. She knew we could leave her there. She didn't beg, she wasn't gesturing at us to lower the ladder, she was just waiting…and hoping. God, the hope. I could see it from the chopper. Looking down at her, looking up at us, I made the only decision I could. I lowered the ladder. I could practically *see* her relief." Benny paused again.

Cookie nodded, knowing how hard of a decision

that had to have been. He waited for his friend to continue.

"To know now some of the hell Fiona went through, and fuck, we both know we don't know the half of it, but to know *some* of what she went through, I feel guilty as hell that I even *thought* about leaving her there."

Silence filled the room, broken only by the slight wheezing noise that Fiona made as she slept on, oblivious to the undercurrents in the room around her.

Cookie nodded at his friend and teammate. "Believe me, I know what you mean. I had Julie all set and we were one step from leaving the hellhole she'd been held in when something made me take one last look around. I didn't hear anything; it was just *something* that made me look again. When I think about if I had ignored that feeling, when I think about how Fiona could have so easily have been left there…" Cookie's voice drifted off.

The men both knew what an extraordinary woman Fiona was. They didn't blame her for what happened tonight. In reality, they both blamed themselves. They should've known she wasn't better yet, they should've been more watchful. But sitting there with Fiona, after watching her anguish and her strength and will to live, they each made a silent promise that nothing would happen to this woman again. No matter where she went, or what she did, they'd keep watch over her. They could do no less.

TWO DAYS LATER, Fiona rolled over with a groan. Her body felt like it'd been through the wringer. She ached all over. Her head felt a little fuzzy, but she took a deep breath and looked around. She saw Hunter sitting in a chair near her bed. His feet were up on the mattress, his arms crossed over his chest, his head canted to the side while he softly snored. Fiona wondered what time it was and why he was sleeping there.

Cookie woke up from his light doze next to the bed to find Fiona staring at him.

"Hi," he said softly, not knowing if Fiona was truly aware of her surroundings or not.

"Hi," Fiona responded. "You look like crap," she told Hunter honestly.

He chuckled. "You don't look so hot yourself," he bantered carefully. His smile quickly left his face and he sat up. He leaned forward and put his hand on her forehead. Fiona tried not to flinch away from him or blush at his gentle touch.

"How are you feeling?" Cookie asked carefully. He wanted to assess Fiona's state of mind before he let her do anything on her own so they didn't have a repeat of her escape out the second floor window.

"I feel weird," Fiona answered honestly.

"How so?" Cookie inquired, tilting his head to the side while he waited for her answer.

"I feel weak, my mouth feels like I've been sucking on cotton for a month, and I have to use the bathroom," Fiona answered honestly.

Cookie just stared at her for a moment.

"What?" Fiona finally asked. "Why are you looking at me like that?"

"Do you remember anything about the last few days?" Cookie asked quietly.

Fiona tensed. Oh shit. What happened? What had she done? She merely shook her head and waited to hear what Hunter had to say.

Cookie looked her in the eyes and merely said, "Okay, I'll help you up and we'll go from there."

Fiona wondered what Hunter was keeping from her, but she really did have to use the bathroom, so the questions could wait. She let Hunter assist her out of the bed and help her walk toward the bathroom. She gestured toward the IV still attached to her arm. "Any chance I can get this out? I'm not a big fan of needles and knowing one is imbedded in my skin, even if it's helping me, creeps me out."

"We'll see," Hunter told her without rancor.

Fiona noticed the door to the bathroom was missing. It actually looked like it'd been splintered from its hinges. She didn't remember a lot about arriving at the house, but she thought she'd remember a missing door. There was no way she was going to pee in front of Hunter though.

"Do you need help?" Hunter asked.

Fiona shook her head vigorously. "No!"

"Okay, I'll be right here next to the door with my back turned. When you're done, just let me know and I'll come in and help you."

Fiona shuffled into the bathroom. Not even thinking Hunter would peek, she quickly did what she needed to do, then turned to the mirror. Oh. My. God. She looked like the creature from the black lagoon. She almost didn't recognize herself. Fiona didn't think she'd made a noise, but suddenly Hunter was there.

Fiona watched in the mirror as he came up behind her and put his hands on the counter on either side of her hips and leaned in. She could feel him all along her back. He dwarfed her. Fiona really hadn't noticed before now how tall he really was. Her head came up to about Hunter's chin. He met her eyes in the mirror.

"How are you *really,* Fee?" he asked quietly.

"I'm okay, Hunter," she told him quietly. And she was. She was alive, she was safe, she wasn't in the jungle. She was fucking awesome.

Hunter continued to look at her. Fiona looked down at the counter. She should've felt penned in with him at her back, but she didn't. It felt…good. She could feel his strength and all she wanted to do was lean on him and let him be the strong one for once in her life. As soon as Fiona had the thought, she dismissed it and tried to stand up straighter. She was strong. She had to be.

Hunter took the choice away from her. One arm came up across Fiona's chest and the other went around her waist. He pulled her back against him. Fiona went willingly. Soon the tears started. She couldn't help it. She was weak and feeling vulnerable. The way he was holding her, as if she was made of glass, was just too much.

Cookie turned her in his arms and held on to Fiona while she cried. He hated to see her so upset, but he was glad to see the honest emotion for the first time since he'd met her.

He wrapped one arm around her back and other around her neck; he tucked her head into the crook of his shoulder. Fiona shook as she cried and Cookie could feel her tears on his neck. Her arms were curled in front of her and he could feel her fingers clutching at his shirt as if they'd never let go.

"Cry it out, Fee. You're safe. I've got you." Cookie murmured the words in Fiona's hair and knew he'd let her stand there all day if she needed it.

"I – I – I don't know why I'm crying." Her words were muffled against his neck, but Cookie still heard her.

"It's relief. I bet you were strong while you were being held, probably wouldn't let those assholes see you cry, but right now you don't have to be strong anymore."

When her tears finally tapered off and Cookie could feel Fiona's trembles subside, he carefully lifted her in his arms and took her, and her IV pole, back into the bedroom.

Cookie set Fiona on a chair in the corner of the room and kissed her on the forehead. He looked her in the eyes and ordered, "Stay put for a bit, Fee. I'm going to change the sheets before you get back in."

Cookie waited until Fiona nodded, then turned to the bed and quickly and efficiently stripped the soiled sheets and put on a freshly laundered set. He wanted to give her time to collect herself. After putting clean sheets on the bed he went back to Fiona and helped her out of the chair. He kept his hand on her elbow and assisted her back to the bed, letting her walk on her own. Cookie tucked her in and leaned down and kissed her on the forehead. He stayed close and whispered, "Sleep, Fee. I'll be here when you wake up again. All is well. I swear."

"Thank you, Hunter. Thank you for finding me. You have no idea, just thank you." Fiona closed her eyes and was asleep again in moments, not waiting to hear

Hunter's response.

When Fiona woke up again, Hunter was there, as he promised. She had no idea how long she'd been asleep. She would've protested Hunter babying her, but if she was honest with herself, it felt good. Hearing a noise near the door, Fiona turned her head and saw Benny was also in the room.

"Hello, Fiona. Are you feeling better?"

"I am. Thank you for all you've done for me."

"You're welcome. It's time for that IV to come out." Benny was all business.

His attitude actually made Fiona feel more comfortable. She never liked being the center of attention.

Benny made quick work of removing the needle from her arm. Fiona rubbed her wrist where the IV had been inserted.

Another man came into the room carrying a tray with food on it. Fiona's mouth immediately started watering. She couldn't even guess when the last time she had real food was. She didn't think it'd be good manners if she snatched the tray out of the man's arms, and fell on it in the middle of the room like she was a starved feline, but, oh, how she wanted to.

"Fee, I want to introduce you to my teammates. That's Dude carrying the tray and Benny took your IV out."

Fiona wrinkled her eyebrows. "Benny? Dude? Are

those your real names?"

Dude chuckled as he put the tray on the bed. "No, Fiona, they're nicknames. Just like Hunter's nickname is Cookie."

Fiona couldn't take her eyes off of the tray. The soup was steaming and the roll sitting next to the bowl looked like heaven. "Ah...okay." She didn't really know what she was saying, the food was taking all her attention.

Benny laughed. "Dude, you'd better back away from that tray, it looks like she'll fight you for it."

Fiona blushed bright red and looked down at her hands in her lap. She felt the bed depress next to her but didn't look up.

Cookie sat next to Fiona, upset that *she* was embarrassed. He put one hand at her waist and pulled the tray so it was in front of him and next to Fiona. "Dig in, Fee, don't mind us."

Fiona didn't hesitate. She grabbed the roll and tore it in half. She didn't bother with the butter which was sitting on the tray, but instead took a big bite of the bread and almost moaned. Jesus, it was even warm. Fiona forced herself to put the pieces of roll down and pick up the spoon. She leaned over so as not to spill the soup all the way down the front of herself, and slurped the delicious broth. It probably came from a can, but it tasted heavenly.

Fiona didn't care that the three men watched her eat, she was starved. When she first saw the food she didn't think it was nearly enough, but after eating half the roll and most of the soup, she was surprisingly full. Fiona knew her body would need time to adjust to eating again. She didn't want to get sick on top of everything else, so she forced herself to put the spoon down.

Fiona felt Hunter's hand at the small of her back and she suddenly realized he'd had it there the entire time she'd been eating. The warmth from his hand felt good. She hadn't been touched gently in a very long time.

Fiona tried to ignore the way Benny and Dude looked at her. She didn't want to try to interpret their looks. She was too tired and too raw for that. Finally, she couldn't stand it anymore.

"I'm sorry," Fiona said with as much dignity as she could.

"For what?" Benny asked, before Cookie could.

"For whatever it is that I did, or whatever happened that I can't remember," Fiona said honestly. She watched as the men glared at each other. "No one has told me anything, but by the way you're all acting, it couldn't have been good. What day is it?" She asked suddenly, changing the subject abruptly. "How long have I been here?" She could tell they didn't want to tell her. Finally Dude gave in.

"Five days."

Five days. Oh crap. "Wow, five days, okay then." Fiona mused out loud. "I must've been really out of it to not remember five days. So again, whatever it is that I did that's making you guys act this way, I'm sorry."

Cookie shook his head. "Fee, there's nothing for you to be sorry about. *Nothing.* Do you hear me?" He waited for her to nod before continuing. "You were sick, we cared for you. That's it."

Fiona knew he was glossing over something, but she let him for now. "Okay." She paused. "Can I take a shower?"

That made the men laugh. "I was just going to ask if you wanted a shower now or later," Cookie told her.

"Oh, definitely now."

Benny and Dude left the room and Hunter helped Fiona out of the bed and steadied her as she swayed on her feet. Fiona looked down at herself and blushed. She was wearing a button down shirt, obviously one of the men's.

Seeing her look of chagrin, Cookie hurried to reassure her. "My shirt was the easiest thing to put you in when you were sick. I can't promise we didn't do anything, but we kept everything as clinical as possible to preserve your modesty."

Fiona just nodded, wishing she could melt into the

floor and never have to see any of the men again.

Cookie put a finger under her chin and forced it up so she was looking into her eyes. "Don't be embarrassed, Fee. We were all worried about *you* and not about looking at your naked body."

"I'm not sure that makes me feel any better."

"Maybe this will then. Even though you've been sick, I still think you're the most fucking beautiful woman I've ever seen."

Fiona's eyes almost bugged out of her head. "Are you kidding me?" She tried to tug her face out of his grasp with no luck.

Cookie put both hands on her cheeks so she couldn't back away from him anymore and tilted her head up even more. His thumbs rested on her lower jaw. Cookie lowered his head until his forehead rested against hers. "No, I'm not kidding. I've never been more serious about anything in my entire life. It's not just your face, Fee, it's you. I don't know the basics about you, your favorite color, where you grew up, or what you like to eat, but I *do* know you. I know you're tough, you have a will of iron, you're compassionate and you have a strong sense of right and wrong. And, most importantly, I know you won't give up. The odds have been stacked against you for a while now, but you just plowed through every obstacle in your way, and when you couldn't bust through it, you held on until you could break through with some help. That's beauty to me, Fee. You're fucking beautiful."

"Holy crap."

Cookie leaned back a fraction and didn't give her a chance to say anything further. "Now, how about that shower?"

Fiona stood in the shower spray enjoying the feel of the water sluicing down over her body. She washed her hair at least three times before she was happy with the feel of it. Hunter had wanted to help her with the shower, saying she wasn't strong enough or steady enough to stand on her own, but Fiona had firmly rejected that idea. It was bad enough he and his friends had seen her naked when she was sick and through whatever it was she'd done.

She stood in the water and for the first time really thought about all that had happened to her. It was all too much; even though she'd had a crying fit around Hunter when she first woke up, she'd been stoic for as long as she could stand. Fiona allowed herself to break down, again. She slid down the wall to the shower floor and sobbed. She cried for what the kidnappers had done to her, the hurts she'd been through, for being scared, and finally for having been rescued.

When her skin was pruned and the shower ran lukewarm, Fiona turned off the water and stepped out, making sure to keep one hand on the towel rack so she wouldn't fall on her face. Hunter had scrounged a T-shirt and sweat pants from somewhere for her to wear. She dried herself off and slipped on the clean clothes. Amazingly, they mostly fit. She didn't have any undies or a bra, but nothing felt better to her than the soft cotton against her skin. She couldn't even remember the last time she'd felt clean. She knew she'd never take it for granted again. She'd probably become obsessed with showering, but Fiona supposed there were worse things to be obsessed about. She shrugged.

Fiona walked out of the bathroom and found Hunter standing to the side of the broken door. He looked strong and fit and his shoulder wound was obviously healed enough for it not to bother her. Fiona had no idea what she should say or do, but she did know somehow he centered her and made the jumpy feeling inside her belly subside.

Cookie stared at the woman who came out of the bathroom. She was still as skinny as ever, and he could tell she'd been crying, but the shower had done amazing things for her. Her skin shone and she looked lighter than she had since he met her.

"You look great," Cookie told her honestly.

Fiona blushed and looked down at her feet. "Thanks, I'm not sure about great, but I feel a hundred percent better."

"Are you still hungry?" Cookie asked her.

"I feel like I'm somehow letting my entire gender down by saying this, but I could eat a cow," Fiona answered honestly. "I was stuffed earlier, but suddenly I'm hungry again."

"I think that'll happen for a while. I know once when my team was on a mission and some of us were captured, once we were released, I didn't feel full for weeks."

Immediately concerned for him, Fiona came toward Hunter and put her hand on his arm. Looking up at him in sympathy, she asked, "How long were you captured?"

"Not nearly as long as I think you were, Fee, but long enough."

"I'm sorry, Hunter."

"I didn't tell you that for your sympathy, but thank you, Fee. My point was, I think you're going to feel hungry for a while, even if you're full right after you eat, twenty minutes later you'll be hungry again. It's your body's way of healing. You'll be better off eating several small meals a day than stuffing yourself with one or two. Just take it easy, your body will tell you when you're done."

Stepping back a foot, Fiona was finding it hard to think straight around Hunter, she nodded at his words. "I'm sure you're right. I've always been a snacker, so it'll be nice to have a reason to snack now."

"Ready to go down?"

At her nod, Cookie took Fiona's hand and they made their way out of the bedroom silently. Cookie held on tight. Everything he'd said to her was what he felt from the heart, but he'd never opened up to any woman like that before. He wanted Fiona. There wasn't one thing about her that turned him off. Not one. If he had anything to say about it, she was his. *His.* He now understood what Wolf and Abe felt about their women. There was something inside him that knew she was meant to be his. He'd have to apologize to both of his teammates for even thinking they were crazy to tie themselves to a woman as quickly as they had to Caroline and Alabama.

Cookie knew he had a ways to go before he'd be able to officially claim Fiona as his. They had a lot to work through, there was a lot he didn't know about her, but at the end of the day, he'd fight to make her his. Forever. She didn't know it, but her life had just changed, hopefully for the better.

Chapter Eleven

WHEN FIONA AND COOKIE entered the dining room, Benny and Dude were waiting for them. The table was set with several bowls filled with delicious smelling food. There were three dishes full of pasta with different kinds of sauce, Alfredo, marinara, and meat sauce, a large bowl of salad, and a plate loaded with corn on the cob dripping with butter. The men had obviously been busy.

Fiona looked away from the food and suddenly felt self-conscious. Obviously, Hunter had arranged for the meal to be served after she was done with her shower, but being around others, she was finding, was awkward, and even a bit uncomfortable. She was the only woman, and was still a bit raw from everything that had gone on while she was held captive.

Cookie noticed her unease and squeezed her hand in reassurance. "Okay?"

"Yeah." Fiona looked up at Hunter as if she'd just thought of something. "You won't leave me will you?"

She meant right then, at the dining room table, but as soon as the words left her mouth, Fiona realized she wouldn't mind if Hunter stayed by her side forever.

Hunter's eyes warmed at her words and he brought their clasped hands up to his mouth and kissed Fiona's knuckles briefly. "Never."

His words and kiss made a shiver work its way through Fiona. Could he read her mind? Fiona relaxed enough at his words to be able to continue walking into the room as if nothing was wrong, but she kept a tight hold of Hunter's hand for extra reassurance.

Cookie was once again impressed with Fiona's inner strength. He noticed the tensing of her body as they'd entered the room, and couldn't help but feel pride at her obvious effort to hold herself together. He knew she'd asked him not to leave her at the table with his teammates, but he'd answered as if she'd asked him if he would *ever* leave her.

Cookie sat Fiona on his left before taking his own seat next to her. There was a feast waiting on the table for them. Fiona couldn't remember seeing that much food in one place before.

"Did you guys make all this?"

Benny winked at Fiona and joked, "It was all us. We're not just pretty faces you know."

"I made the salad and boiled the corn," Dude told Fiona seriously, continuing to answer her question

143

about the food, "but Benny is the chef. I've never tasted anything he's made that hasn't been downright delicious."

Benny just shrugged and commented nonchalantly, "I like to cook."

The meal was lively with everyone joking and kidding around. It was interesting to be in an atmosphere like that for Fiona, as she'd never had a big family and didn't really know how to act. She mostly just smiled at the other men and joined in the conversation when she could. She knew this happiness wouldn't last for her though. First of all, she couldn't stay in this house forever. Fiona wasn't even sure where she was; just that she wasn't in Mexico. Fiona knew she had to get back home sooner rather than later, and she figured the guys did too. This was but a short moment in her life, and she had to enjoy it while she could.

Fiona also figured, at some point, she was going to have to talk to Hunter and his team about what had happened to her, but she wasn't going to bring it up unless they did.

After finishing the meal, and eating less than she thought she would considering how hungry she'd been when she walked into the room and had seen the food, Fiona helped Hunter and the others carry the dishes into the kitchen. She insisted on helping put the dishes into the dishwasher and pack away the leftovers. The men had put up a token protest, but in the end had allowed her to help.

While Fiona kept a good distance from Dude and Benny, she noticed Hunter was by her side almost the entire time they were in the kitchen. Every now and then he'd put his hand on her waist to guide her to the side, or to get her out of the way of one of his teammates. His hand felt possessive, but in a good way. Hunter was true to his earlier word not to leave her side.

Later that evening, Fiona sat on a couch with Hunter sitting next to her and Benny and Dude across from them in two easy chairs. They were in the library, one of the most comfortable rooms in the house. Fiona knew the guys did it deliberately, giving her room and not crowding her, but she was still on edge.

"Want to watch TV, Fiona?" Dude asked.

Fiona thought about it for a second. It'd been forever since she'd last seen any kind of news, and she suddenly had a violent urge to see what had been going on in the rest of the world since she'd been kidnapped. "I'd love to watch the news…if that's okay?"

"Of course it's okay. No problem." Dude leaned over and snagged the remote that was sitting on the small coffee table. He clicked on the television and flicked the channels until he came to a twenty-four hour news station.

Fiona watched, completely enthralled, as she caught

up on the politics and other news stories she'd missed out on.

Cookie kept his eyes on Fiona, gauging her mental state as she stared at the TV. Cookie didn't think about how she would feel, missing out on everything going on around the world, but it was obvious she was enjoying catching up.

Seeing Fiona gasp, Cookie turned to look at the television, just as Benny snatched the remote off the table where Dude had thrown it and turned the volume up.

Our next story comes from Washington DC where Senator Lytle held a press conference to discuss the rumors that his daughter, Julie Lytle, had been kidnapped. Let's tune in…

Before I get into the details of what happened to my daughter, I just want to publicly thank the members of the SEAL team that were dispatched into Mexico to rescue my daughter. The men and women of our armed forces are unsung heroes, and they risk their lives every day fighting against evil all over the world. Sex trafficking is a problem that is not only a United States issue, but it's a problem all over the world. Women and children are being kidnapped, and forced into prostitution and slavery and forced labor. I'm going to use my position to lobby our government to do something about it. Now, as for the rumors, my daughter was…

The television went dark as Benny clicked it off.

Fiona turned to look at him eyebrows raised in question.

"You don't need to relive it."

Fiona simply nodded. If she'd thought about it a bit more, she probably would have been very uncomfortable listening to whatever Julie's dad had to say about Julie's time in captivity. It was the right move on Benny's part.

"With that being said, can you tell us your story, Fiona?"

Fiona swallowed, it looked like it was time. She couldn't put it off anymore.

"Tell us who you are, Fiona," Cookie coaxed gently. "How did you end up in that hellhole and where do you come from?"

Fiona took a deep breath, knowing her time here in this sanctuary was coming to an end. They wouldn't kick her out, but she had to go back to the real world, *her* real world, and they had to go back to rescuing people. It was what it was.

"My name is Fiona Rain Storme." She watched the men cringe, then struggle to hold back their grins. "Yeah, horrible isn't it? My mother was fourteen when she had me...and she told me it was raining cats and dogs when I was born. Apparently the storm was sudden and unexpected. She'd planned to give me the middle name of Sarah, but when the storm came on right when she was heading to the hospital, and with her last name already being Storme, she decided to change it. I admit, it's not very creative, but I'm sure it seemed so to a teenager. I never knew my father; he was long gone before my mother had me. We lived with my mom's parents for a while, but it was obvious they didn't like her, or me. She was kicked out of the house when she was eighteen, and I was four. We moved around a lot, staying in homeless shelters and stuff until I was about eight. Then one day my mom never came to pick me up from school. I sat in front of the building until eight at night when one of the teachers who'd left work late, saw me and called the police. I never saw my mom again. I have no idea what happened to her and I've come to terms with that. I went into the foster care system because my grandparents didn't want me…but it was fine."

"Fine?" Cookie asked sternly.

"Yeah, fine."

Cookie knew he hadn't even heard the bad part of her story, but he was so pissed off at her mom and grandparents, he was barely holding himself together. But to hear Fiona describe her childhood and the foster care system as "fine" almost pushed him over the edge.

"What exactly does 'fine' mean to you Fee? I know how you've held up with the things that happened to you in Mexico and I suspect you'd probably downplay those to others and describe them something like 'no big deal.' So, I want to know exactly what 'fine' means to you."

Fiona looked at Hunter. He didn't look happy. She'd sworn to herself when she'd turned eighteen and gotten out of her last foster home that she wouldn't use it as a crutch or an excuse for anything bad that happened in her life. She definitely didn't want these beautiful, bad ass men to think she needed coddling, or worse, to feel sorry for her.

Ignoring the other two men in the room for the moment and taking a risk, Fiona leaned toward Hunter and put one hand on his knee and leaned her head against his shoulder. She wouldn't have to look at him this way, but it also served the secondary purpose of comforting her. Not entirely surprised, Fiona felt Hunter's arm immediately wrap around her shoulders and he pulled her closer into him and shifted until she was more comfortable.

When Fiona didn't immediately answer, Cookie prompted her. "Fee?"

"It just means that while it wasn't a fairy tale childhood full of ponies and hearts and flowers, it wasn't the hell that a lot of kids go through."

Fiona felt Hunter nod and press his lips to her hair. "Okay. For now. Can you tell us how you got to that hellhole in Mexico?"

Fiona took a breath, knowing this was the hardest part to tell. "I currently live in El Paso. I work as an administrative assistant at a local University. It's a perfectly boring job and I lead a boring life. I spend most of my days trying to help students register for classes or dealing with mad parents and students. I was getting burned out and I needed to take a break. I was on vacation in Florida when I was taken."

Fiona paused again, not really wanting to tell the guys how stupid she'd acted. She wanted nothing more than to call her story done and never think about it again, but she owed these men. They'd risked their lives to help her. She felt obligated to tell them. Fiona felt Hunter put his free hand on top of the one that was resting on his leg. He squeezed it reassuringly. It was amazing how much she relied on his small touches. Fiona didn't know why she could tolerate Hunter's touch, when the thought of any other man touching her as Hunter was, freaked her the hell out, but she was too tired to analyze it. Fiona took a breath and continued.

"I went on vacation alone. I'd convinced myself I was an adult and it was perfectly fine and safe for me to travel on my own. No one would be interested in bothering me. I'm not gorgeous or the type of woman predators would be looking for. I'd been there three days, not really enjoying myself, if you must know. It's not that fun to be by yourself on vacation. I went to restaurants by myself, I even went snorkeling by myself, but it's not very exciting when you can't share your experiences with anyone."

"Why'd you go by yourself in the first place, Fee?" Cookie asked gently, not understanding how someone like Fiona could be so alone.

Fiona looked down, embarrassed.

"Jesus, I'm sorry, I didn't mean to embarrass you," Cookie told her; mortified his innocent question had caused her even a second of awkwardness.

"It's okay, Hunter. I was tired of my job. It's not that exciting or interesting and I just wanted to take a break. I don't have any close girlfriends that I would've felt comfortable in asking to go with me."

Dude asked the question that Cookie had been dying to ask, but had bit back. "Do you need to call anyone and let them know you're all right? That you're alive. Boyfriend? Husband?"

Fiona picked her head up off of Hunter's shoulder and looked up at him in alarm. Even though Dude had asked, she spoke to Hunter. "Oh my God, no. I'm not with anyone. I wouldn't…I didn't…" She started to sit upright, mortified Hunter might have thought she was married or had a boyfriend and was leaning against him so intimately.

Cookie gathered Fiona back into his arms and held her tight. He could feel her trembling. "Shhhh, Fee. No one thought anything inappropriate. Relax." He caressed her back and glared at Dude.

Dude just shook his head in exasperation. "Yeah, Fiona, I just wanted to make sure you knew you could contact anyone you needed to."

Fiona pulled away from Hunter just enough so she could turn her head and look over at Dude. "There isn't anybody."

At her anguished words, Cookie put his hand on her head and pushed it back into his chest. He loved feeling Fiona's arms hesitantly curl around his body, holding him back. "Tell us the rest, Fee. You're safe here. Go on. Get it all out."

Fiona nodded against Hunter's chest, not lifting her head. "Okay, so anyway, it was my fourth day in Florida and I was leaving the next day. I decided I should at least check out a club once when I was there."

Hearing Benny snort, Fiona laughed, but it wasn't with humor. "Yeah, dumb. I know. So in I went, by myself, thinking I was all that and more. I had a few drinks and watched others dancing. A guy asked me to dance, I said yes; when it was over I went back to the bar and continued drinking my drink."

Again, when Benny snorted, Fiona agreed with him. "Yeah, I know. Again, I was dumb. Really dumb. Seriously dumb. No one knows that more than me. I paid for it. Big time." The room got quiet. No one said a word, knowing what Fiona would say next.

"When I woke up, I was in that room Hunter found

me in. I was still wearing the stupid T-shirt, shorts, and flip-flops I'd worn to the club. I suppose I should be glad I wasn't wearing heels, that would've made it really hard to tromp through the jungle. I'm not sure how many days had gone by when I woke up, but I was pretty out of it. They must've started the drugs before I came to. I was chained by the ankle at first, but when I attacked them whenever they got close to me, they wised up and chained me by my neck. They could control me better that way. I figure I was there for about three months, but it was probably more based on the time that I was out of it." Fiona paused. No one said a word, although she could see Dude and Benny clenching their teeth.

"What did they want you for?" Dude asked finally, knowing, but wanting to see what Fiona would say.

"They wanted to sell me as a sex slave, but I wasn't 'properly trained,'" Fiona told the men without tempering her words. "They were waiting for me to break. To beg for mercy, to beg for more drugs, to beg to die…something. But I refused. I wouldn't give in to them. They couldn't steal who I was. And I figured whatever they had in store for me would be worse than where I was, so I refused them. I don't think they would've kept me as long as they did, but they didn't know what else to do with me at that point."

"Good girl," Cookie muttered, stroking Fiona's hair.

"They were getting more and more pissed though," Fiona continued, ignoring Hunter's comment for the moment. She'd think about it again when she had time to reminisce about sitting there in his arms. "I think their buyer was getting desperate. He wanted his sex slave and he wanted her now, that's when Julie showed up. She was way different than me, so I was a bit confused. I figured their buyers would want a certain 'type' of woman, and Julie wasn't anything like me in looks or temperament. But maybe the guy was desperate and didn't care anymore. If you guys hadn't shown up when you did, Julie would've been gone soon. She caved the second they put her in the room. She begged to be let go. She went along with everything they told her to do, thinking her cooperation and 'Daddy' would save her. She was so freaked out and scared and plia-ble…they were going to sell her in a few days. Then I think they were going to kill me."

Benny couldn't hold back anymore and asked the question both he and Cookie were wondering. They'd talked about it together while she'd been recovering and couldn't figure it out.

"Why didn't you say anything when Cookie came into the room? You weren't so out of it with the drugs that you didn't know he was there, were you? Were you really going to let him walk out and leave you there?"

Fiona thought about how she wanted to answer

Benny, but she didn't know exactly what they were looking for. She could've said all sorts of things, but she did what she usually did, she told the truth, looking up at Hunter when she answered. "You weren't there for me. It wasn't fair of me to lower your chances to get out of there with Julie alive. No one had paid to get me out. I don't have any family, no close friends, I was weak and I knew it. Something had changed with the kidnappers. They hadn't fed me in a couple of days and had even stopped giving me the drugs. They were tired of dealing with me and since they had Julie to sell, I think they were just going to leave me there, chained to the floor, to die. I figured it was better if one of us got out, rather than neither of us."

No one said a word when Fiona stopped speaking.

Fiona shifted on her seat. Hell, that had sounded dramatic, even to her. Christ. She was pathetic. "So…." she started.

"Shut. Up," Cookie said harshly, enunciating each word clearly. He was breathing hard through his nose; clenching the hand he'd laid on Fiona's leg so hard, his knuckles were white. His touch was gentle, but he looked like he was about to burst.

Dude stood up and paced the room. Fiona could hear him muttering under his breath, but she couldn't make out what he was saying.

Finally Cookie couldn't stand it anymore. The

words burst forth. "Jesus, Fiona. How in the hell did you walk fifteen miles in flip-flops and shorts through the jungle, half carry me to that ladder, carry a backpack weighing a hundred pounds and cling to a rope ladder after being chained to a floor for over three months, being drugged against your will and having not eaten for who knows how long? Oh, and let's not forget, you were fucking *shot* while clinging to that damn ladder!"

Cookie's voice had steadily risen as he'd spoken and he disengaged himself from Fiona carefully and stood up. Fiona sat up as he moved. He stalked away from her, changed his mind when he got halfway across the room and stalked back. Cookie knelt in front of Fiona, not touching her, his eyes boring into hers. His hands rested on his thighs while he waited for her to answer his semi-rhetorical question.

Fiona stared back at him. Mesmerized by his eyes, not caring that Benny and Dude were in the room with them. She gave Hunter the only thing she could. "Because if I didn't, you probably would've died in that jungle trying to get me and Julie out," Fiona told him quietly, with one hundred percent sincerity. "If it was just me, I would've just laid down and died. I'm not strong like you are. It didn't matter. Don't you get it? *No one was looking for me.* I have no family, no real friends. It. Didn't. Matter. Then you came to rescue Julie and I knew you wouldn't leave me behind. Oh, I thought you might at first, and I was hoping you would, but at the same time scared you'd actually leave me there. I wanted to scream out when you started peeling back that board in the hut. I heard you loud and clear. I would've rushed across the room if I could've."

Fiona took a breath, but didn't look away from Hunter. His body was coiled with an emotion she couldn't read. She continued, trying to explain. "The first time you looked at me like I had two heads when I asked if you'd take me too, I knew you were the kind of man that would never leave someone behind. So I trudged along behind you, mile after mile, thinking about how bad *you'd* feel if I just keeled over. That you'd think it was *your* fault. So I didn't. I couldn't. I ignored how crappy I felt. I ignored how much I hurt. I concentrated on making it, one step at a time, counting down one number at a time until we were either rescued or killed."

Cookie stared at the woman sitting in front of him for another second or two, then stood up and walked out of the room without another word.

Fiona looked down at her fingers, which were cold. She'd been clutching them together tightly throughout her explanation to Hunter. She looked up at Benny and Dude. Benny had a weird look on his face that Fiona couldn't interpret.

"What?" she asked him defensively. "You would've

done the same thing," Fiona told him almost accusingly.

"You're right," Benny answered without hesitation, "and Dude would too, but we're men honey. And SEALs. Trained. And I'm not sure either of us could've done it in the same circumstances."

Fiona shook her head. "Yes, you would," she said softly. "You know you would."

Benny and Dude continued to look at her. Fiona figured now was her chance to ask about what had gone on when she was out of it. She didn't want to think about Mexico anymore. Hunter's reaction to what she'd said was freaking her out. Was he disgusted, pissed, upset? She had no idea. She was nervous without him by her side, so she tried to change the subject.

"Please tell me what happened this week. What did I do that I don't remember?"

"How do you know anything happened, Fiona?" Dude asked back. "How do you know you didn't just lie on that bed out of it for the last five days?"

Fiona sighed. "I wasn't sure, but you just proved it. Please, Dude. I need to know."

The guys really didn't want to tell her, but she deserved to know. Dude looked at Benny, and saw him nod slightly.

Dude told her the basics of what had happened. He glossed over the part where she fought them and what she specifically said, but it was enough to make her pale a bit and bite her lip.

"I really am sorry. I-I-I didn't…"

Benny interrupted her. "You have nothing to be sorry for, Fiona. If you must know, we all admire you."

Fiona looked at Benny as if he was crazy.

"We do. You were clearly outnumbered, and there were three of us, and still you fought. You're strong, Fiona. You don't give up. That's a great trait to have."

Fiona wasn't sure what to say. She just looked down at her hands again. She was glad she didn't remember it, but Jesus, she'd really climbed out of a second story window to try to escape? She probably had. If she'd had the chance back in that hut in Mexico she would've done whatever she had to in order to get away. Even if that meant setting off into the jungle by herself.

"Come on, Fiona, you look exhausted. I'll take you back to your room so you can sleep." Benny came over to where she was sitting on the sofa and held out his hand.

He was big, but as Fiona came to know them, she knew they'd never hurt her. She grasped his hand hesitantly and stood up. As soon as she was steady on her feet, Benny let go of her, knowing she wasn't comfortable with casual touching yet, and gestured toward the door.

Benny escorted her back to the bedroom they'd brought her to the first night she came to the big house.

The room was just as she remembered it. Big and white. The bed looked very comfortable. It was a big four poster bed that was about three feet off the ground. It even had a little step stool next to it to help people get into it. The comforter was fluffy and looked super soft. Even with her body crying out for sleep and the fabulous looking bed, Fiona didn't think she'd be able to sleep.

Remembering the look on Hunter's face when she talked about what happened to her, was killing her. She didn't know if he was mad, disgusted, impressed, or what. It was stressing her out. She supposed it didn't really matter in the long run. They now knew who she was, they knew where she lived, and that she was alone in the world. Fiona also knew she'd soon be going home. She had a life, Hunter had a life. It was time they got back to it.

Chapter Twelve

TWO HOURS AFTER Cookie had abruptly left Fiona and his teammates in the library, he opened Fiona's bedroom door a crack and peered inside. He'd tried to stay away from her, he really did, but he couldn't. He'd spent the last eight days with her; Cookie actually couldn't sleep well now without her. Even when Fiona had been out of it, he'd slept near her, holding her hand and talking to her.

After listening to her story tonight, Cookie wanted to immediately go back to Mexico and kill every single one of her captors. They were going to leave her to *die* in that pit. Perhaps worse than that, was that Fiona knew it. She would've starved to death, and no one would've known. It would've been a slow agonizing death. If she'd been left there, Cookie never would've met her. Never been awed by her strength. Hell, he might not have made it out of the jungle alive if Fiona hadn't been there to help him make it to the ladder so his teammates could haul him up to the helicopter.

Cookie couldn't imagine not knowing Fiona. He honestly didn't understand how she'd made it out of her entire situation alive, and amazingly well.

He knew the human body was resilient, but Fiona was amazing. And humble. That was what got him. How the hell had Fiona grown up so humble and unassuming? Her so-called mother certainly hadn't instilled it in her, and while she hadn't told them what she'd been through in her childhood, they'd all been able to put some of the pieces together. Being a foster kid was never a picnic, and certainly not for a teenager.

Fiona honestly had no idea that what she'd done and lived through in Mexico was extraordinary. She did it because it had to be done. Period. She didn't want praise, and in fact was embarrassed by it, but she did it anyway. Fiona told her story matter of factly, whereas most other people who'd been through the same thing, would be in hysterics.

Cookie closed the door silently behind him and made his way to the bed where Fiona lay. He wasn't completely surprised when she turned over to look at him in the moonlight coming through the window.

"Couldn't sleep?" she asked softly.

Cookie just shook his head and motioned for her to scoot over.

Fiona did and watched as Hunter took off his T-shirt and let his sweats fall to the ground. He was gorgeous. In the moonlight, Fiona could see the scars on his chest, but he was built like a brick wall. Hunter was muscular, and the play of his muscles in his arms was sexy as hell. He had a light sprinkling of hair on his chest and she could see his biceps flex as he moved. His thighs looked strong and she could tell he was big…all over.

Before Fiona could take a more concentrated look at the part of him that interested and scared her, he climbed into the bed. Without a word, Hunter ran his hand over her head and brought it toward him. He kissed her briefly, too briefly, on the forehead then encouraged her to turn on her side, facing away from him.

Fiona felt Hunter snuggle up behind her as soon as she turned, pulling her back to his front. His arm came around her chest, holding her tightly against him. She sighed and snuggled deeper into his embrace. Fiona knew she should probably be freaking out that Hunter had stripped naked before joining her in the bed, but she'd felt safe when he'd held her this way back in the jungle, and she felt safe now. His skin was warm and Fiona could feel his heat soaking into her body. She wasn't thinking about what her kidnappers had done to her, and knew Hunter wouldn't push her into anything she wasn't ready for. She might never be ready, but Fiona hoped that wasn't the case. She wanted to be intimate with a man again, with this man.

"Are you okay, Hunter?"

"I'm sorry I left."

"Don't be. I understand. *I'm* sorry I upset you."

Cookie tightened his arms and put pressure on Fiona's hip until she turned onto her back. He came up on one elbow and his other hand came up to her face and cupped her cheek. Fiona had no choice but to look at him.

"*You* didn't upset me. Those assholes that kidnapped you upset me. I'm so damn proud of you I could burst. You have no idea what you mean to me." He saw the confusion in Fiona's eyes. "I know, I'm laying a lot of heavy stuff on you, but I want to be upfront with you about how I feel. Can you take it right now?"

Fiona stared at Hunter. He was leaning over her and his hand had moved from her face to brush her hair behind her right ear. His fingertips were tracing her ear, sending shivers throughout her body. She wanted to press herself up into him, even with all that happened to her, she wanted that.

"Fee?"

Oh yeah, he'd asked her a question. "I can take it." She bit her lip and looked up at the man she was beginning to think she couldn't live without. She hoped she could take it, but if Hunter needed to tell her something, she'd listen, no matter if she was ready or not.

"I know it's probably too soon, but I've never felt this way about a woman before. I've always been the one to walk away. I know I've been a jerk in the past. But I don't want to walk away from you. The thought of you being hurt, or killed, makes me crazy. The thought of walking out of this house and never seeing you again, makes me crazy. The thought of your body under mine, makes me crazy." Cookie eyed Fiona nervously. He had to finish his thoughts and stop beating around the bush.

"You're mine, Fiona. I know that makes me sound like a fucking caveman, but I can't apologize for it. I want to protect you. I want to show you off. I just want you. In every way." Cookie closed his eyes and leaned his head down and put this forehead against Fiona's. He could feel her warm breath against his face. He lowered his voice. "I know you have some stuff you have to work through, and I want to be there with you while you do it. All I want is a chance. A chance to show you that you're safe with me. That you'll always be safe with me."

Fiona's breath hitched. Hunter's words were like band-aids on her soul. All she'd ever wanted since she'd been in her first foster home was to feel safe and wanted. Hunter was offering her both.

"I…"

Cookie placed a finger over her lips lightly. "No,

don't say anything, Fee. I know this is fast. Probably too fast, but I know what I want, and that's you. Sleep on it. Don't agree because I want it. Agree because *you* want it. There's more we have to talk about tomorrow, stuff that's pretty heavy, but know that I'll be there with you." Cookie looked down at Fiona. He had no idea how this woman had survived what she had, but there was no doubt in his mind that she was his. He just hoped she might want that too. "Turn back on your side again. Let me hold you?"

Fiona did as he asked without hesitation. She wanted Hunter to hold her too. When she turned over, she felt Hunter curl up into her again. His bottom arm was between them, curled up against his chest and against her back. His other arm was curled over her back and he pulled her against him by placing his hand against her breastbone.

Fiona could feel the heat from his hand against her breast. She felt a moment of panic, before consciously relaxing. This was Hunter. She was safe with him.

"I want you, but I'm scared." she whispered as if saying the words out loud would make them have less power over her.

"I know you are. I'll never pressure you, Fee. I want you, you can feel that, but know that I'll never force you. I'll wait as long as you need. Okay? I won't tell you not to feel scared, but while you are, know that I'm here and I have your back. You don't ever have to be scared of *me*."

Fiona nodded. She *could* feel how much he wanted her. His erection against her butt was long and hard. She wished she could turn over and show him how much his words meant to her, but he was right. She needed to take things slow. Colossally slow.

"Thank you for coming to me tonight." There was more Fiona wanted to say, but those were the only words she could get out.

"You're welcome, Fee. I'll always come to you if I can."

Fiona nodded and snuggled back into Hunter's arms.

Cookie lay with Fiona throughout the night. He didn't sleep. He couldn't. Twice when she started having a nightmare, he woke her up slowly and soothed her until she fell back asleep. She was human. She might've been able to somehow make it out of the jungle alive, but she was affected. Deeply. She might always be, but Cookie knew Fiona would show a brave face to the world and fight her demons behind closed doors.

It's the same thing he'd always done. Cookie loved this woman. He didn't know how it had happened so fast, but it had. He wasn't going to let her go. He wasn't sure what their future had in store for them, but he wasn't going to let her slip away. Finally, around dawn, Cookie fell into a light slumber, holding Fiona tight and wondering how to make her want to stay with him…forever.

FIONA WOKE UP alone the next morning, but when she turned over she could see the indentation from Hunter's head in the pillow next to her. She looked around, and seeing she was alone, picked up the pillow he'd used, and held it to her face. God, it smelled good. It smelled like Hunter. Fiona put the pillow down and stared at the ceiling.

It was time to think about going home. She didn't want to, but she didn't have a choice. She figured that was what Hunter meant when he said they had to have a serious conversation today. Fiona was sure the men had to get back to their base by now as well. It wasn't as if they could stay here forever.

After showering and putting on a pair of sweat pants and a T-shirt that had been left in the bathroom for her, Fiona made her way down the stairs.

She walked into the kitchen to see all three of the guys sitting at the small table, obviously waiting for her.

"Hey, guys," Fiona said cautiously.

Hunter got up and came over to her and enveloped her in his arms. Fiona buried her head in his chest and wrapped her arms around him.

"Good morning, Fee," Cookie said softly, his rumbly voice making her feel mushy inside.

"Good morning, Hunter."

He pulled back and looked down at her.

"Hungry?"

"Uh, yeah," Fiona couldn't help the sarcasm that escaped with her words. She watched as Hunter threw his head back and laughed.

"All right, come on, Benny made us all a gourmet breakfast."

Cookie pulled away, but took Fiona's hand and led her to the small table. He waited until she was seated before heading to the refrigerator. "Orange juice okay?"

"Oh my God. Yes. Please. I haven't had OJ in…well, a long time."

Cookie took a deep breath. Jesus, Fiona slayed him with her words and she had no idea. He filled a large glass to the brim and brought both the glass and the container of juice to the table. If Fiona wanted juice, she'd get as much as she could drink.

The four of them sat around the table and enjoyed the pancakes and omelets Benny had made for them. They were mostly silent during the meal, the men thinking about the upcoming conversation they had to have with Fiona, and Fiona thinking she'd never had anything half as tasty as the food she was currently eating.

After they'd finished, Fiona grabbed her plate and stood up, intending to take her dishes to the sink.

"No, sit, Fiona," Dude practically barked at her.

She startled badly and almost dropped her plate.

"Shit, sorry. I didn't mean to scare you." Dude's tone of voice was placating and apologetic.

"No, it's all right. It's me."

"Bullshit. I was rude, and I'm sorry. What I meant to say, was leave the plates. We can do the dishes later."

Fiona nodded. She should've noticed before now, but all three of the men seemed tense. Was this it? Were they going to kick her out now? Was she going to have to say good bye to Hunter?

"We have to talk."

Fiona almost moaned at Benny's words. Yup. It was time. "It's time to go isn't it?" She might as well get the ball rolling.

Cookie took hold of Fiona's hand and held it tightly against his thigh. "Yes. But we have some stuff we need to talk to you about first."

Cookie didn't want to tell Fiona what Tex had found out for them. But she was right, it *was* time to go. They had to get back to base and Cookie wanted Fiona with them when they went.

Benny took over the conversation from Cookie. "Okay, so this house isn't ours. We have a friend, a

arms and let her cry.

Fiona heard a chair scrape against the floor and then felt another hand on her back. She turned her head to see Benny kneeling by the chair.

"You were an at-will employee at the University, hon. Unfortunately, legally they *can* hire someone to take your place." He went on, obviously answering her earlier question. "Tex is trying to track down your stuff. Your landlord had to do something with it. If it's still around, Tex'll find all of it for you. As for your bank account, most of your bills were being auto-drafted, and when your money ran out, they started bouncing. But don't worry; Tex is taking care of that for you as well. You won't owe anyone a dime once he's done."

Cookie nuzzled Fiona with his chin and she turned to look up at him. "Come back to California with me," he repeated, this time he ordered the words instead of asking them.

"But…"

"No, no buts. You heard what I told you last night. I wish I could say I'm sorry you lost your job and lost your apartment, but even if it makes me a dick, I'm not, because that means you're free to come with me, to be with me, to start over in California. I'll be honest, until we talked to Tex, I had no idea how I was going to let you walk out of this house and away from me. I have to go back. I don't have a choice, but I knew you had a life. If you can honestly tell me you want to go back to El Paso, I'll help you any way I can. But know that I don't want you to. I want you with me."

Fiona tried to focus on what Hunter was telling her. She'd heard him last night, but she obviously didn't *hear* him.

"I'm scared."

"I know you are, Fee, and that's why I'll be right there with you. Trust me."

Without pausing, Fiona immediately returned, "I do. Jesus, Hunter, I think I trust you more than I trust myself right now."

"Then come with us. Let me introduce you to Caroline and Alabama. Let the rest of my team get to know you. You'll come to trust them as much as I hope you trust me."

Dude cut in, he and Benny hadn't left the room. "You have choices, Fiona."

"What the hell, Dude?" Cookie barked out immediately, tightening his arms around Fiona protectively and glaring at his teammate.

"She has to know she has options, Cookie. If you really want her to go with you for the right reasons, you have to tell her all her options."

"Tell me." Fiona was ninety nine percent sure she wanted to go to California with Hunter, but Dude was right. She needed all the information she could get so she could try to make the right decision.

"Your bank account can have as much money as you need by the end of the day. Don't ask how, just know that Tex can make sure you have the money you need in order to rent another apartment and get settled again. He's probably already arranged to get your car out of the impound lot where it was towed from the airport parking lot. If you want to keep working for the University, Tex can arrange that too. While they were legally in their rights to replace you, it'd be a public relations nightmare if it came out you were kidnapped and the school dumped you. They'll be begging you to come back and work for them once Tex gets done with them."

"He can do that?"

"Hell yeah," Benny told her seriously. "We don't know how he can do the things he does, but we're just damn glad he's on our side."

Cookie turned Fiona's head back to him. "As much as I want to beat the crap out of Dude, he's right. You need to know you can go back to El Paso and get your life back. If you choose that option, just know it won't be the end of us. I'm not letting you go, no matter what you decide."

Burying her face into Hunter's chest, Fiona whispered, "Really?"

"Really. I already told you you're mine. It doesn't matter if you're living in Timbuktu, Texas, or in the same house as me."

Fiona looked up at Hunter and nodded.

Apparently that was all the reassurance the guys needed. "I'll call Tex and tell him to get us home," Dude said decisively as he got up from the table.

Benny also got up off the floor where he'd been crouching, and started gathering the dishes from the table. "I'll clean this up. Tell Tex we'll be ready to go this afternoon."

Cookie stood up with Fiona in his arms and without a word, headed for the door. Benny watched with a small smile as they left.

Chapter Thirteen

FIONA SHUT HER eyes and enjoyed the feeling of Hunter carrying her. She kept them closed until she felt him bending over. She finally opened them to see he'd brought her back to the room they'd slept in the night before. He carefully leaned over and placed Fiona on the mussed sheets, then put both hands next to her shoulders and loomed over her.

"I need to touch you, Fee." Before she could say anything, Cookie continued. "We won't make love; I know that'll take time. You need to heal physically and mentally before we go there, but I have to hold you. I have to feel you against me. You said you trusted me before. Please, let me show you that trust isn't misplaced. Let me show you how much you mean to me."

Fiona could only give him a small nod. She wanted to feel him too. As much as she wanted to be ready to take him inside her, she knew Hunter was right about her mental state. It was way too soon.

She watched as Hunter stood up and put one hand

behind his head and yanked his T-shirt off over his head. Fiona would never understand how guys learned how to do that. Throwing his shirt behind him carelessly, Hunter began to unbutton his pants. He never took his eyes off of hers.

When Fiona began to sit up to take her shirt off, Cookie quickly said, "No, let me. Please."

Fiona lowered her hands back to her sides and continued to watch as Hunter stripped off his clothes.

Cookie kept his eyes on Fiona's face as he unzipped his pants and lowered them. He was hard. There was no way he could control his body's reaction to Fiona lying on a bed in front of him.

"I don't want you to feel vulnerable, Fee. I'll do whatever it takes so you're comfortable with everything we do." Cookie put his thumbs in the waistband of his boxers and quickly stripped them down his legs and off. "Scoot over."

Fiona knew she was blushing. Hunter was the sexiest man she'd ever laid eyes on. He'd stripped off all his clothes so she'd feel more comfortable, but she wasn't sure that was what she was feeling. She wanted to touch him. She wanted to lick him. She wanted to snuggle in next to him and never let go. Fiona scooted over in the large bed and watched as Hunter climbed in and reached for her.

Cookie tried to control his lust. Having Fiona in

bed with him, awake and willing, was almost more than his libido could handle. He'd never felt this hard and aroused in his life. Before reaching for Fiona, he needed to hear the words from her.

"Tell me you're okay with this, Fee. I need the words."

"I'm more than okay with this, Hunter. I want to touch you."

"I'm yours. Do whatever you want."

Fiona reached a shaky hand toward Hunter. He was lying on top of the covers, completely bare. His chest had a light smattering of hair and she could see scars covering the surface. Fiona lightly placed her fingertips on one of the worst scars. Hunter sucked in a breath and Fiona yanked her hand back.

"I'm sorry, did that hurt?"

Cookie grabbed her hand and pressed it back to his chest. "Hell no, it didn't hurt. Your hands on me are a dream come true."

Fiona let her hand wander over his chest, fascinated at Hunter's reaction. She kept her eyes above his waist for now, but watched as goose bumps rose over his body. As she stroked his scars, his nipples stood up on his chest. She had no idea a man's nipples got hard like a woman's. Without thinking, Fiona leaned down and took one in her mouth.

"Jesus, Fee. God yes. Shit, that feels so good. Suck

hard…just like that."

Fiona could feel herself getting wet. She'd never gotten excited in the past without having a man's hands directly on her, but this was Hunter. He was completely different from any man she'd ever been with.

Cookie resisted the urge to put his hand on Fiona's head and press her deeper into him. He hadn't planned on his happening, he wanted to make *her* feel good, but now that she was touching him, he was helpless to stop her. When she switched to his other nipple he almost lost it.

"Touch me, Fee. God, please."

Fiona raised her head and looked down for the first time. Hunter was big, bigger than anyone she'd been with. She could see the blood pulsing in the vein on the side of his shaft. Hearing Hunter plead with her was heady, and almost wrong. She didn't want him to have to beg her for anything. It just wasn't right. She reached for him and wrapped her hand around him. She swiped her thumb over the tip and smeared the wetness she found there over and around the head.

"Fee, harder, hold me harder."

Fiona felt awkward for the first time. Hunter obviously needed something, but she wasn't sure what. "Show me."

Cookie immediately uncurled his hand from the sheet he'd been holding and wrapped it around Fiona's on his shaft. He showed her how hard to grasp him to make it as pleasurable as possible. He knew he was much rougher than she would've been. He threw his head back and closed his eyes.

Fiona watched Hunter in awe. He was so beautiful. She loved how he took control of his pleasure. Yes, her hand was around him, but he was clearly in charge and showing her how he liked it. When his head went back she leaned down and took his nipple into her mouth again and sucked hard.

Cookie groaned at the feel of Fiona's tongue on his nipple and when she sucked, he lost it.

"Fee, I'm gonna…" Before he could finish warning her, Cookie felt her teeth bite down on his nipple. He exploded into their hands and thrust up as Fiona continued to grip and stroke him and nibble on his nipple. Cookie shuddered and thrust one more time as another mini-orgasm went through him. He felt completely drained.

Cookie let go of her hand and let his fall to the bed with a plop. He shuddered as Fiona continued to stoke him lightly and finally she let go, only to run her hand up his body until she was massaging his release into his abs.

"You're beautiful," Fiona breathed as she stared down at Hunter. Without thinking, only knowing she wanted to taste him, Fiona brought her hand up toward her face.

Cookie caught her hand just as she got it to her face. "You wanna taste me, Fee?" At her tentative nod, he took his free hand and wiped it over his stomach, collecting some of his cum. He bought it up to her face and held one of his fingers out for her. "Taste me."

Fiona tried not to blush and leaned over and took Hunter's finger into her mouth. The taste of his salty and earthy essence filled her. She swirled her tongue around his finger, making sure to clean it thoroughly. Fiona watched through lidded eyes as Hunter's pupils dilated and he drew in a deep breath.

Fiona was surprised when Hunter suddenly surged toward her and took her mouth with his. She wouldn't have dreamed in a million years that a man would want to taste himself, and she knew he could. Fiona felt his tongue wrap around hers. They both voraciously ate at each other. After several moments of the best kiss of her life, Fiona pulled back. They stared at each other. Fiona looked away first and glanced down. He was still semi-hard. She'd forgotten about the mess they'd made.

"I should get a towel to clean you up."

"No. Don't. I want to feel you against me. I have a need to mark you. Does that freak you out?"

Fiona could only stare into Hunter's eyes and shake her head.

"Jesus, you own me, Fee. Seriously. You're perfect."

Cookie looked at Fiona for a moment then fingered the hem of her T-shirt. "Do you think you can take this off for me? We won't go any further. Just your shirt."

Fiona wanted this. She didn't hesitate. She sat up and grabbed the bottom of her T-shirt and whipped it over her head quickly so she wouldn't chicken out.

Cookie didn't hesitate, giving Fiona a chance to get freaked out, and grabbed her hips and eased her over him so she was straddling his thighs. She was still wearing sweat pants, but he could only stare. She wasn't wearing a bra, and Cookie had an unfettered view of her chest. Her breasts were perfect. He'd always thought his "type" was a woman with a huge chest, but Cookie realized in that moment Fiona was the perfect size for him. Her areolas were large and took up most of her breast. She had pink nipples that were currently hard and reaching for him. She was a bit small for her size, but Cookie figured once she gained the weight she'd lost while in captivity, they'd grow a size. He didn't care. The bottom line was that they belonged to his woman, therefore, they were perfect.

Cookie picked up her hand that had caressed him earlier, and placed it on her own right breast. He made sure Fiona wiped his release on herself. Then he took both her hands in his and placed them on his hips.

"Hang on, Fee. Don't move your hands. I won't go too far, I promise. But I need to do this." Cookie didn't wait for her to agree, but maintaining eye contact, took both his hands and smoothed them over his belly, collecting his essence that she'd coaxed from him earlier. Once they were coated, he brought them up to her chest slowly and touched his woman for the first time. He finally broke eye contact and looked down. Cookie caressed and massaged Fiona, all the while branding her with his scent, with his very being.

"You're mine, Fee. No one else will touch this. No one else will get to see this. I'll protect you with my life if I have to. You're safe with me. Mine. You're mine."

Fiona couldn't hold back her sob any longer. She'd realized what he meant to do the second he put his hands on himself, and she wanted it. She wanted to feel him on her skin. It was as if his hands and cum washed away the feeling of the kidnappers' hands on her. When he'd said she was his, she lost it.

Fiona collapsed on top of Hunter, knocking his hands off of her chest in the process. The feel of his chest against hers only made her sob harder. She'd needed this kind of connection for so long. She vaguely felt Hunter's arms against her back, pulling her into him and soothing up and down her spine. Fiona wasn't afraid of Hunter, she wasn't afraid of what his hands would do to her. Being in Hunter's arms felt right.

After a long crying session, Fiona picked her head up, but Hunter wouldn't let her separate their bodies any more than that. She looked into Hunter's eyes and said what was in her heart. "Yours."

Fiona watched as Hunter's lips curled up in a satisfied smile. "Damn straight."

She smiled back, feeling content for the first time in a long time.

"Do you want to shower or sleep?"

"Do we have time?"

"Yes."

Showering meant washing his scent off. The decision was easy. "Sleep."

"Damn, woman." Cookie breathed, putting his hand on the back of Fiona's head and pulling her back into his embrace. "I love that you don't want to wash me off. Sleep then. We'll shower when we wake up. After we shower, we need to be heading out. You *are* coming back to California with me aren't you?"

Fiona could hear the insecurity in Hunter's voice and hated it. She didn't want him to be insecure about her or the relationship they were obviously starting. She hurried to reassure him. "Yes. If I have to start over I'd rather start over in the same place where you are so we can see if whatever this is…" she gestured between them, "…will last."

"Oh, it's gonna last, Fee. You're not getting away from me," Cookie said it with a smile, but he obviously meant every word. His sincerity rang out loud and clear in his voice.

"Thank you, Hunter."

"You don't have to thank me, Fee."

"I know you think that, but I do. I'll never stop thanking you as long as I live."

"As long as you aren't confusing what we have here, with gratitude."

Annoyed, Fiona propped herself up. "Seriously? After what just happened? You think that was a thank you hand job?"

"Shhhhh. No, I don't think that." Cookie put one hand on the side of her head and stroked her hair. "I just…hell. I'm gonna sound like a teenage boy here, but I just want you to be with me because you want to, not because you don't feel like you have another choice or because you're grateful."

Seeing Hunter insecure and unsure was actually kinda cute, even if she didn't like being the cause of it. Fiona knew it wasn't something she'd see very often. It was her turn to reassure him. She brushed her hand over Hunter's head to the back of his neck and put her forehead against his. "I'm here because I can't imagine being anywhere else. Even when I was out of my head with the drugs, I think I knew you were here next to me. Well okay, maybe not when I crawled out the bathroom window. But I hoped you might ask me to go home with you even before I knew about my job and apartment." At the look of satisfaction in Hunter's eyes, Fiona giggled. "Does that make you feel better?"

"Yeah, sweetheart, it does. Now, come down here and close your eyes. We'll have to get going here soon enough, but for now I just want to lie here and enjoy being with you."

Fiona closed her eyes as he asked and settled against his chest. They were sticky and it was a bit uncomfortable, but it was real, and it was a part of him. She'd stay right where she was forever, if it meant he'd be there with her.

Chapter Fourteen

Benny, Dude, Cookie, and Fiona headed toward the exit of the airport. Tex had gotten them all a commercial flight out of the Dallas/Fort Worth airport later that night. Identification was waiting for Fiona when they'd arrived at the ticket counter, as if by magic.

Cookie could only shake his head in wonder. Tex was amazing. Cookie had no idea how Tex did half the stuff he did, but he thanked his lucky stars for the millionth time that Tex was on their side. How they managed half the stuff they did without him, Cookie would never know.

"Remember, Fee, Wolf and Caroline will probably be waiting for us out in the main part of the airport. We told him we were coming back and he couldn't wait to see for himself that you were all right." Cookie kept hold of Fiona's hand to reassure her.

Fiona was quiet. She barely remembered the man Hunter called Wolf. She knew he was there in the helicopter and later, but she'd been barely hanging on, and didn't really recall anything they might have said to each other.

As the foursome exited the secure part of the airport and entered the main terminal, Fiona saw a group of people standing off to the side. Fiona knew instinctively they were waiting on them. There were three large, almost scary looking, men, and two striking women.

Benny and Dude made a beeline for the group, but Cookie pulled Fiona to a stop well away from his friends. He turned her to him and took both her hands in his. "If you don't want to meet them now, it's okay, just let me know and we'll go and get a taxi back to my place. I want you to meet them when you feel comfortable with it."

Fiona squeezed Hunter's hand. God, he was so good to her. "It's okay, Hunter. I want to meet them. I *need* to meet them. They all had a part in saving me."

Cookie brought Fiona's hand up to his mouth and kissed it briefly. "Strong as hell," he murmured under his breath, then turned them both toward his teammates and friends.

As they got closer and Fiona could see the men better, she realized she did recognize them. She didn't know who was who, but she recognized them.

One of the women detached herself from one of the men and came right up to them.

"Oh my God, we are so glad you're here! I'm Caroline and that big lug back there is Matthew." At the look of confusion on Fiona's face, Caroline sighed dramatically. "Yeah, okay, you've been hanging out with them…" she gestured toward Benny and Dude, "…so you probably have never heard everyone's *real* name. Alabama and I try not to use their nicknames, we prefer to call them by their given names. So Matthew is with me and he's Wolf. Standing over there are Alabama and Christopher, or Abe. You know Benny and Dude, but Alabama and I call them Kason and Faulkner. Then, last but not least, is Sam, who's known as Mozart by the guys."

Fiona's head spun. She'd never remember all their names.

As if reading her mind, Caroline laughed. "Don't worry if you can't remember. It took me for-freaking-ever to keep them all straight. It's like there are twice as many of them around when the guys are using their nicknames and we're using their real names."

Fiona could only nod as Caroline continued talking. "So, I haven't heard much of what happened, only that you were kidnapped and rescued in Mexico and that you were awesomely strong. At least that's what Matthew told me. I'm so happy you're all right. Will you be staying with Hunter? Do you have clothes? I'm happy to…mmmmf."

Fiona smiled as Wolf came up and put his hand

over Caroline's mouth. "Jesus, Ice, give the woman a chance to breathe."

"Ice?" It was the only thing that immediately came to Fiona's mind.

Hunter leaned down close to Fiona's ear and explained, "Yeah, Caroline earned that nickname when Wolf first met her. It's a long story, and one I'm sure you'll hear sooner rather than later the way Ice talks, but for now maybe we can get the hell out of here?" He directed the last part of his words to his friends.

"Of course. Got any bags?" Mozart asked Cookie, Benny, and Dude.

"Naw, Tex arranged for our stuff to be shipped. You know how it is," Dude said, while winking at Fiona.

Fiona knew they probably couldn't have brought their bags on the plane with them since they were loaded down with weapons and who knew what else.

"Great. You and Fiona are with us, everyone else is with Wolf," Abe said, chiming in for the first time.

Fiona took a look at the woman at Abe's side. She'd been quiet, but she was very watchful. She hadn't taken her eyes off of Fiona since they'd walked up. It made Fiona extremely nervous. She'd never been good at making friends, and she really wanted these women to like her. Fiona knew if she had a chance at making whatever it was she had with Hunter work, she had to get along with his teammates' women.

Before they all left, Caroline ducked out of Wolf's hold and hugged Fiona tightly. Fiona couldn't help but stiffen in the embrace. Caroline held up her hand when Hunter took a step into Fiona. "I know, I probably overstepped my bounds there, but I'm so happy you're here and with Hunter. He deserves the best, and from the little I've heard, that's you. I can't wait to sit down and get to know you better. Alabama and I need someone new to gossip with."

"Jesus, Ice. Get out of here," Cookie scolded with a laugh, grabbing Fiona's hand and pulling her back into his side, with his hand around her waist and resting on her hip.

Caroline laughed with him and stood on her tiptoes and kissed Hunter on the cheek. "Don't keep her all to yourself, Hunter."

Cookie just shook his head as Caroline and the other men headed toward the exit. "Come on, Fee, let's get you home."

Home. Fiona liked the sound of that.

The four of them headed out the doors of the airport and Abe led them through the parking garage and over to his jeep. Alabama and Abe got in the front and Cookie helped Fiona climb into the back before heading around to the other side and climbing in next to her.

When they were on their way out of the parking area, Alabama turned sideways in her seat and spoke up for the first time.

"Fiona, I'm so glad you're all right. Christopher told me a little of what happened and I can't imagine what you've been though." Her voice was quiet and soothing.

"Thanks, Alabama. I appreciate it. I'm glad I'm all right too." Fiona smiled at the woman in the front seat. She seemed to be the complete opposite of Caroline, quiet and reserved, but Fiona liked her immediately.

"As Caroline said, if you need anything, please don't hesitate to call one of us. It can be tough being with a SEAL and we need to stick together."

Abe spoke up at that. "Hey, we're not so bad."

"Uh, yeah, sometimes you are," Alabama disagreed.

They both laughed. Fiona smiled. They seemed to be at ease. If she'd met any of the men on Hunter's team alone in a dark alley, she would've been terrified, but meeting them all together and seeing how close they were, made a huge difference.

"Thanks, Alabama. I'm sure we'll have lots of time to hang out." They smiled at each other.

The four made idle chit-chat as Abe made his way to Hunter's apartment. Pulling up, he didn't turn off the engine, but turned around in his seat to look at Fiona.

"I have to echo what the others have said, Fiona. You don't know how happy we are that you're okay. I was there, I know what I saw. Thank you for saving Cookie's life. You have no idea what that means to all of us. You're family now. You need anything, all you have to do is ask. I don't care what it is. You want a car? Just ask. You need money? Same thing. If you need a lawyer, an ear, or a way to get out of Cookie's place, we're only a phone call away."

"What the hell, Abe?" Cookie growled from next to Fiona.

Abe held up his hand to forestall anything else Cookie might say. Fiona could only look between Hunter and Abe in confusion. She thought they were friends. Why was he saying that about Hunter? Was he warning her away from him?

"I'm not insinuating you'll want to get away from him at all, Fiona. Out of all of us, Cookie is the most sensitive, and, dare I say it, caring. But I'm trying to make a point here. I learned my lesson with Alabama and the mistakes I made. My team stepped up when I let her down. I learned the real meaning of family. Family supports and trusts each other unconditionally. You aren't alone anymore, Fiona. Hell, if someone hasn't heard from you in two hours, we'll start trying to get in touch with you. Understand? *You're not alone.*"

Fiona got it. She could only nod. If she tried to talk, she'd burst into tears. No one in her old life had noticed or cared that she'd disappeared without a word. Abe was telling her that wouldn't happen here. She didn't even know these people, but they'd showed more compassion to her than anyone had since she'd been a kid.

"Come on, Fee, let's go home."

Home. Jesus, that sounded great. Fiona nodded at Hunter then turned toward Abe and Alabama. "Thanks." It was all she could say at the moment through the huge lump in her throat, but it seemed to be enough.

Cookie opened the door on his side of the jeep and didn't let go of Fiona's hand. She had to scoot across the seat so she could follow him out.

"Thanks, man. See you later." Fiona watched as Hunter and Christopher gave each other manly chin lifts to communicate non verbally, then she was being tugged toward the apartment building. She looked back once to see Alabama lean over and kiss her man passionately. Fiona smiled. She hadn't said more than a few words to the woman, but she liked her.

They stopped in front of a door on the second floor. Cookie turned her so they were facing each other. "I'm gonna apologize now before we get inside, Fee. I recently moved out of the barracks and the apartment isn't fully furnished yet." At her raised eyebrows, Cookie continued. "Okay, so there isn't much in there except for a bed, a sofa, and a huge-ass television, but whatever you need or want, we can get. Okay? Don't freak out."

Fiona laughed. "Hunter, Seriously? I don't care. I just spent three months in a damn hut in the middle of a fucking jungle in Mexico. Whatever you have is more than I have right now and it's a million times better than where I was. It's fine."

Cookie hated being reminded of the hell Fiona had been through, but understood her point. Trying to keep things light, he mock grumbled, "I'm gonna remind you that you said that when you see it and are bitching about how it's the ultimate bachelor pad."

Cookie took the keys out of his pocket and unlocked his apartment door and watched as Fiona entered his home. He watched as she glanced around the living area. It wasn't much, as he'd warned. The leather sofa was comfortable as hell, and of course the fifty four inch TV took up most of one wall. Otherwise it was pretty plain. There were no pictures on the walls and Cookie hadn't even bought a carpet to put down on the hardwood floors. There was no hall table and no knick knacks sitting around. Hell, Cookie could even hear an echo as Fiona walked across the room.

He watched as she went straight to the sliding glass door that opened to a balcony. Fiona pressed her hands against the glass and looked out without a word. Cookie locked the front door and threw the keys onto the counter as he walked past the kitchen to get to her. Cookie put his arms around Fiona's waist as he came up behind her.

"What are you thinking, Fee?"

"This is the most amazing view."

"It's why I chose the apartment. There were bigger ones in the complex, but I liked the idea of being able to sit on the balcony and have a beer or eat dinner, and seeing both the beach and the mountains at the same time in the distance.

Fiona turned in his arms and laid her cheek against Hunter's chest and snuggled into him. "It's beautiful. I didn't think I'd ever see anything like this again. I thought…"

"Shhhh, I know."

They stood glued together for a long time. Finally Cookie pulled away. "Come on, Fee, let's head to bed. We're going to have a long couple of days coming up. We need to get you settled, and I need to make sure you have what you need. If I know Caroline right, she's gonna show up here as early as Wolf will let her out of the house. She'll want to take you shopping."

Fiona looked up at Hunter and nodded. She *was* tired. She couldn't think of anything she wanted or needed more at that moment, than to cuddle up next to Hunter in his bed. How the hell she could want that, after everything that happened in Mexico, Fiona had no idea, but there it was.

Cookie's thoughts were much the same as Fiona's. He wanted to see Fiona in *his* bed. Not a borrowed bed, not on the ground in the middle of the damn jungle, but on *his* sheets in *his* home in *his* bed. Call him a Neanderthal, but he needed that.

Chapter Fifteen

COOKIE WAS RIGHT. There was a knock at the door at ten o'clock the next morning. Luckily they'd been up and ready. Cookie looked out the door and saw it was indeed Caroline, but he was surprised to see Alabama with her. He opened the door and welcomed the ladies inside.

"I'm surprised Wolf let you out so early, Ice."

"Ha, ha, very funny, Hunter. You know he forced me to stay away until now. I wanted to be here at eight."

"Oh, I'm sure he didn't have to 'force' you, Ice." Cookie laughed when Caroline blushed.

"Yeah, well, maybe he didn't have to convince me too hard."

"I bet it was hard."

Fiona laughed out loud at the comical way both Hunter's and Caroline's heads whipped around in shock at Alabama's words.

"It's always the quiet ones you have to watch out for," Fiona said, still laughing.

Caroline came up and wrapped her arm around Fiona's waist. "I like you, Fiona. I think you're gonna fit right in with us. You ready to go and spend some money?"

At her words and actions, Fiona stiffened. Shit. She wanted to spend some time with them, but she didn't *have* any money.

Seeing Fiona's body go tight, Cookie swore under his breath. He should've talked about this with Fiona already. "Can I talk to Fee for a second, Ice?" Cookie didn't give Caroline a chance to agree or disagree, and grabbed Fiona's hand and tugged her into the kitchen.

When Fiona opened her mouth to speak, Cookie covered it with his hand lightly. "Listen to me for a second, Fee. Remember when I said you were mine?" Waiting for her to nod, Cookie continued. "This is a part of what that means. I have money. I have too much money. Look around. I live simply, I have few obligations outside of my duty to my country. I have *plenty* of money, and you spending it on clothes and other odds and ends won't even make a dent."

Fiona twisted her head to dislodge Hunter's hand over her mouth. He let go immediately. "I don't like taking your money, Hunter."

Cookie sighed. "How did I know you were going to say that? Okay, here's the deal. Remember I told you about Tex?" When Fiona nodded, Cookie went on.

"Well Tex is good at what he does. You're not broke anymore, Fee." When she just stared at him incomprehensibly, Cookie tried again. "Tex is a computer genius. It's almost scary the things he can do. He arranged it so you're not broke. You aren't rich, but you aren't broke either."

"Are you saying he put money in my account…" Fiona's voice dropped to a whisper as if the police were somehow listening and would barge in and demand to know where Tex was so he could be arrested, "…illegally?"

"I don't think I'd put it that way. But let's just say he decided it wasn't right that you got fired so he *arranged* it so the money you would've made over the time you were in Mexico, was deposited into your account…plus interest."

"But, I can't take that money either, Hunter. It's not right."

Cookie sighed and tugged Fiona into his arms. It seemed he was always pulling her into his chest, but he loved the feel of her there and it didn't seem to bother her. "Believe me, Fee, we've tried to rein Tex in, but he does whatever he feels is right. If you pay him back, he'll turn around and do something bigger. Believe me, we've tried. After Tex used his contacts to find where terrorists had taken Caroline, Wolf sent him a bouquet of flowers, knowing it was lame and not very manly to send a former SEAL flowers, but not knowing how else to thank the man. Wolf sent it as a tongue-in-cheek thank you, but Tex turned around and ordered two dozen roses to be delivered *every day* for two weeks to Wolf's house. We've all learned that a simple 'thank you' is enough when it comes to Tex."

"Kidnapped by terrorists?" Fiona said incredulously.

"Focus, Fee," Cookie jokingly admonished. "It's either my money or yours."

"I can't use illegal money."

"Then please, take my card today. You won't bankrupt me. I promise. Even if Caroline takes you to Louis Vuitton and you buy the place out. Okay?"

"Do you even know who Louis Vuitton is?"

"Fee…"

Fiona nodded. "Okay, okay, but I'm keeping all the receipts and if I get too much I'll take it back."

Cookie just shook his head at Fiona. She was unbelievable, in a good way. Every girlfriend he'd had in his life had jumped at the chance for him to pay their way. Fiona was unusual in every way. "Kiss me before we go back out there. I need you."

Fiona stood on her tiptoes and didn't hesitate. She reached for Hunter as soon as the words were out of his mouth. It wasn't an easy kiss; it was raw, and sensual as hell.

Cookie devoured Fiona's mouth. He held nothing

back. He wanted Fiona to know how much he needed and wanted her. Even if it was years before she'd be psychologically ready to make love with him, he'd wait however long it took.

Fiona felt goosebumps shoot down her arms as Hunter kissed her. He made love to her mouth. His tongue thrusting in and out mimicked the act of making love. Hunter tasted her, ran his tongue over her teeth and curled it around hers intimately. Fiona felt one of his hands move under her shirt and up her back.

His hand was rough and warm. The goosebumps that were on her arms, moved to her legs. As Hunter's tongue melded with her own and pushed into her mouth, his hand moved around to her side and pulled her closer into him. Fiona felt his thumb brush against the side of her braless breast, then move a fraction of an inch to brush once over her nipple. It immediately puckered at his touch. Just as Fiona arched her back to encourage Hunter to continue, Caroline called from the other room.

"Come on you two! Don't start anything you can't finish in there! I'm ready to shop!"

Fiona startled badly and pulled back with a gasp.

Cookie swore under his breath, but didn't let go of Fiona.

"Easy, Fee. It's okay." Cookie could feel her breathing hard, whether it was from being startled or from their actions, he wasn't sure. Cookie didn't immediately move his hand. Fiona was soft and warm and he wanted nothing more than to take her shirt off and worship her breasts with his mouth. He wished he'd done it before, but he knew they'd have all the time in the world to get there.

"I wish you'd go without a bra every day, but I suppose that's going to be your first stop isn't it?" Cookie laughed as Fiona blushed. "Relax. Caroline won't come in. We'll wait here until you're ready."

"If you don't move your hand, I might never be ready." Fiona laughed at herself.

"I like my hand here."

"I can tell."

They stood there looking at each other for a heartbeat before Cookie slowly moved his hand away from her breast and down to her waist. "Be safe today, Fee. Caroline and Alabama have my cell number if you need anything. Don't be afraid to ask them to call me. I'll pick up a cell for you today while you're shopping. I'll put you on my plan. And before you ask, it won't cost that much to add you. Get what you need and what you don't need. You have no idea what it means to me to know you're walking around in clothes that I paid for. It's Neanderthal, but it's the way I feel."

Fiona blushed and laughingly pushed at him. "You man, me woman." She teased.

"*My* woman," Hunter countered semi-seriously.

Fiona just shook her head and stood on her tip-toes to kiss Hunter quickly on the lips. "I'll call if I need you. I'll see you later?"

"You'll see me later."

Cookie held Fiona's hand as they walked out of the kitchen and back into the hall where Alabama and Caroline were waiting for them.

"Jeez, you guys are worse than me and Matthew ever were."

"Uh, no they aren't," Alabama countered immediately. "I remember me and Christopher once waited for you guys for twenty minutes and finally just left without you because you got distracted and ended up back in bed."

Fiona giggled as Caroline blushed. She'd have to remember not to get on Alabama's bad side. It seemed the woman had a way of remembering and throwing dead-on one liners like no one she'd ever seen.

"Anyway, let's go! I haven't been shopping in like a week!" Caroline tried to get the conversation off of her and her own sex life and back on shopping.

Everyone laughed and they headed toward the door. Fiona looked back as she left and saw Hunter standing right where he'd been when they made it back to the hall. Their eyes met and he winked at her and mouthed, 'I'll see you later."

FIONA SLUMPED ON the sofa in Hunter's apartment. Jesus, she had no idea what she'd been in for when she'd left that morning with Caroline and Alabama. She figured she'd have to rein Caroline in, but Alabama was the one that took control of their shopping. She'd dragged them from one store to another. They'd filled their cart with all sorts of clothes and the other women even insisted on including sexy undies and bras. When Fiona was ready to call it quits, Alabama insisted they visit "just one more store." Of course that one store turned into five.

Fiona had spent way more money then she'd planned on. She was going to buy an outfit or two, some jeans, T-shirts and some nice utilitarian cotton undies and bras. When she'd said as much to Alabama and Caroline, they'd objected strongly, then just ignored her wishes for the rest of the day.

Fiona had *known* it was the quiet ones she had to watch out for. Alabama was no push-over, no matter what her first impression might make someone think. When they were jostled by a man who wasn't watching where he was going, Alabama tore into him and he'd fallen all over himself apologizing before he'd slunk away.

After shopping, Caroline and Alabama brought Fiona to a place called *Aces Bar and Grill*. They said it was the team's favorite bar and that they went there all the time to have lunch, or dinner, or even for drinks at night.

They had a lunch with no nutritional value, but was delicious. The other women introduced her to a waitress named Jess, who they said was always there and was, in their words, awesome. In between serving the other patrons, Jess laughed with them and told them some funny stories about some of the other regulars who made asses out of themselves on an almost nightly basis.

Fiona had asked Caroline what was wrong with the pretty waitress, as she noticed she walked with a limp, but Caroline had just shrugged and said they'd never asked.

After being gone for most of the day, the women had finally taken Fiona back to Hunter's place. It was amazing how tiring a day of shopping and laughing could be.

Fiona closed her eyes and felt herself relax. She'd get up in just a second and see what she could make for dinner. Fiona knew Hunter would be hungry when he got home, and she wanted to do something nice for him. After all, he'd done a ton of nice things for her lately and Fiona wanted to make sure Hunter knew she appreciated him.

Cookie closed the door loudly behind him. He didn't want to surprise Fiona and scare her in the process. When he didn't hear anything, he walked carefully into the living room. He didn't see Fiona, but he did see a ton of shopping bags strewn about. He smiled. God love Caroline and Alabama. He knew they wouldn't let Fiona skimp on shopping. He had to be the only man alive that loved knowing his woman had just spent a fortune on clothes and other feminine fripperies.

He came around the side of his couch and smiled even brighter. Fiona was sprawled on the couch fast asleep. Her head was to the side and one of her arms was flung out and hanging over the edge. Cookie sat down next to her hip and massaged her back. He wanted to wake her up slowly so she wouldn't be scared.

"Fee? Wake up, sweetheart." Cookie kept rubbing her back, but put a bit more pressure on her. "Come on, sleepyhead. Have you eaten?"

Fiona slowly came awake. Without opening her eyes she knew Hunter was there with her. She could smell him, not to mention the goosebumps his hand on her back was raising. She pried one eye open and looked up at him.

"I'm awake. What time is it?"

"About seven. You hungry?"

"Oh shit!" Fiona sat up so quickly she barely missed knocking her head into Hunter's. She didn't even notice, but continued with her tirade. "I was going to make dinner for you! I'm so sorry, Hunter! What do you want? Are you hungry?"

"Whoa, slow down, Fee. You don't have to make me dinner. I'm thrilled I'll get to make it with you. I've never really done that before."

Fiona looked up at Hunter. "Really?"

"Really."

"But I wanted to thank you for all you've done for me. And I just wanted to…you know?"

"You thank me every day by being here with me. By being mine. But I do know. I want to do things for you every day too. Tell you what, if you don't ever feel bad for not having dinner ready when I get home, I'll let you do it every now and then."

"*Let* me?"

"Yup. Let you."

They smiled at each other. Cookie held out his hand and helped Fiona to her feet.

"I'll compromise with you, Hunter. I'll cook dinner with you if you help me decide what of this crap Alabama and Caroline forced me to buy today I should keep and what I should return," Fiona told him seriously.

"That's easy, keep it all."

"Hunter, you haven't even *seen* any of it."

"I don't have to. If those two forced you to buy it, I know it looks great on you."

Fiona just shook her head. "You're insane."

Cookie kissed the top of Fiona's head and sauntered into the kitchen. "Insanely happy you're here with me."

FIONA STOOD AWKWARDLY next to the bed. Hunter was already in bed and had a sheet covering his lap. Fiona knew he was naked under it and she so badly wanted to throw back the covers and attack him, but knew she wasn't going to.

She'd worn the new nighty the girls had insisted she buy, along with the matching pair of panties. Even though she was adequately covered, Fiona still felt mostly naked. She hesitated next to the bed, not knowing if she should slip into the bed next to Hunter with her nightgown on or if she should take it off.

Hunter decided for her, holding out his hand. "Come here, Fee."

Fiona put one knee on the mattress and went to lay down. Hunter grabbed her arm and pulled. She fell against him and quickly got under the sheet and stretched her legs out until they tangled with his.

Cookie could feel Fiona's heart beating hard against his chest. "Relax, sweetheart. You're safe."

"I don't know what to do."

"You don't have to do anything. Just be here with me. We'll figure it out together. Okay?"

"Okay."

After a few minutes, Fiona wiggled against Hunter. She could feel the hair on his legs rubbing against hers. It should have brought back bad memories, but instead all she could think about was the other night when he'd exploded in her hand.

Fiona slowly moved her hand against his chest, remembering the feel of Hunter's nipples hardening under her ministrations.

Cookie lifted a hand and put it over hers on his chest. "I love your hands on me, Fee, but I want to pleasure you tonight. Will you let me?"

"I don't know if I can."

"How about we take it slow, and if I do anything that makes you uncomfortable, I'll stop."

Fiona nodded. "I trust you, Hunter."

"I won't betray that trust." Cookie moved one hand up to the back of Fiona's neck and leaned up and over to kiss her. He kept the kiss light, not wanting to spook her. He used his other hand to swipe up and down her body, gentling her. He kept his touch on top of her short nightgown, which had ridden up to expose her panties, not delving under it. He could feel Fiona squirming under him. Finally when she moaned, Cookie moved his hand so just his fingertips skimmed under the front panel of her panties.

"Do you know how good you feel, Fee? You're so soft. You were meant for my hands. I can't wait to taste you. I bet you taste so sweet. You'll explode so hard when I put my tongue on you, won't you?"

Fiona shivered at his words. God Hunter felt good. His words were making her crazy. "Please, Hunter. Please." She had no idea what she was begging for, but she needed something. She needed more.

"What do you want, sweetheart?"

"More."

"More? More of my kisses? My hands on you?"

"Yes. All of it."

Cookie loved making Fiona feel like this. He didn't really want her to beg, but he also wanted to make sure she wanted it, wanted *him*. He moved his fingers back and forth just under the waistline of her panties. He could feel the heat coming from her core. He leaned down and kissed her again and moved his hand so it was covering her mound, but on top of her panties.

Cookie rubbed against Fiona while kissing her, his tongue mimicking the movements of his hand. He ground the heel of his hand against her clit and couldn't deny the pleasure her cry of delight gave him.

Fiona threw her head back and grabbed hold of Hunter's wrist while he moved his hand against her.

Cookie stilled, not knowing if she wanted him to continue, or stop.

"Don't stop. God, don't stop."

He grinned. Thank God. Cookie rubbed against

Fiona harder and harder while alternating kissing her face and nibbling on her neck.

"That's it, Fee. Rub against me. You feel so good, you're so hot. You're doing fine. You're so sexy."

Cookie could feel Fiona was getting close. He'd been keeping his groin away from her, not wanting to freak her out, but now he let himself brush against her.

"Feel how hard I am. You did this. You're so sexy. I'm going to come with you, Fee. Just watching you get off makes me lose it. Feel me."

He let go of her neck with his other hand and brought it to her chest. Cookie tweaked a nipple that was already sticking up through the fabric of her nightgown. At the same time, he leaned down and blew into her ear then sucked the lobe into his mouth hard. "Come for me, Fee. Come now."

Fiona shattered. Her back arched and she cried out in ecstasy. She couldn't remember the last time she'd orgasmed that hard...or if she ever had. She could barely remember her own name, nevertheless anything or anyone that came before Hunter. When Fiona came back to reality, she could feel Hunter's face against her neck and he was breathing hard. She also felt wetness against her hip.

"Whoa."

Cookie chuckled. "Whoa indeed. Just watching you made me lose it too."

Fiona opened her eyes and stared into Hunter's eyes which were locked onto hers. "You did?"

"I did. Your smell, the feel of your heat. It's all so damn sexy, I couldn't help it. When we get together for real, we're going to be fucking combustible. We won't get out of bed for days."

Fiona could only smile up at Hunter. His words made her relax. He didn't think she was a freak, and apparently he really *didn't* want to rush her into a deeper intimacy she knew she wasn't ready for.

"Come on, as much as I love my mark on you, you can't sleep in that wet gown." Cookie climbed out of bed, completely unselfconscious about his naked body. He went into his closet and Fiona heard him calling back to her. "Where'd you put your nighties? I want to see you in the red one."

"The second drawer on the left," Fiona called back, completely floored Hunter was getting her a new nightgown to wear. She'd never been with a guy that had bothered to take care of her in any way after sex.

Fiona watched as Hunter came back into the room.

"Come on, climb out."

Fiona pulled the sheet back and climbed out, embarrassed by the wet splotch covering the front of her gown. Why she was embarrassed, she had no idea, especially considering she wasn't the one who left it there.

Cookie grinned at her. God she was cute. "Arms up."

Fiona closed her eyes and did as Hunter told her. He'd just made her come, it didn't matter if he saw her naked, and he'd seen her boobs before as well. It wasn't anything he hadn't seen a million times on other women either. At least that was what Fiona tried to tell herself.

Cookie tried to keep his touch as clinical as possible. He took hold of the bottom of her soiled gown and pulled it over her head. He could feel his heart speed up. He wondered for the millionth time how she'd survived the hell she'd been through down in Mexico. She seemed way too fragile to have been able to come through it at all.

"Keep your arms up, Fee. Give me a moment and I'll have you covered in a second."

Knowing he couldn't prolong dressing her, no matter how much he might want to, Cookie put the red nightgown over Fiona's head and pulled her arms through the straps. It fell over her hips with a swoosh. Now for the hard part.

Once the gown was covering her hips and fell to mid-thigh, Cookie grabbed hold of her undies and slid them down her legs without warning her, keeping her covered the entire time.

Fiona squeaked as she felt the underwear fall down to her ankles.

"Step out, sweetheart. I've got a new pair for you. These are soaked." Cookie kept his voice low and controlled and unthreatening.

Fiona did as Hunter asked, knowing she was bright red.

"God, I love it when you blush. I think the red goes from your face all the way to your toes," Cookie teased, trying to keep Fiona's mind off of what he was doing. He tapped each ankle when he wanted her to step up and was able to get the new pair of panties into place. He couldn't resist running his hands over her butt cheeks and down the back of her thighs before he stood up.

"Come on, back to bed."

They crawled back into bed, and it didn't escape Fiona's notice that Hunter took the side of the bed that had the wet spot. She snuggled back into his arms and sighed.

"What was the sigh for?"

"I'm so happy. It's hard to believe two weeks ago I was…"

"Don't finish that sentence."

"But…"

"I don't want to picture you there again. It kills me."

"It's okay, Hunter. I was just going to say that I don't think I've been happier in my entire life and in some warped way, I'm glad I was kidnapped, if only because it brought you to me."

"Jesus, Fee. I can't…I don't…"

It was Fiona's turn to shush him. "It's okay, Hunter. I won't bring it up again, I swear."

That night Cookie woke up once again to Fiona having another nightmare. Not one night went by without her dreaming about her captivity and he fucking hated it. She never talked about it, but Cookie knew she had to talk to someone. She wasn't moving on from her experience as well as she could, as evidenced by the nightmares she still had every night. It wasn't healthy and as well as Fiona was doing, Cookie knew she'd break if she didn't get it out. As much as he wanted to be the one she talked to, he knew he had to get her to a professional. He'd seen a lot in his life, but he didn't think he'd be able to handle what she'd say about her time in Mexico. If she needed to tell him, he'd listen, but if not, he *never* wanted to hear it. He knew what happened to women who were taken, destined to be sex slaves, but he couldn't think about his Fee being in that situation.

Cookie soothed her as best he could, and held her as she cried. As usual, Fiona never fully woke up, but settled back into his arms without a word as he counted out loud to her. Cookie always started at a hundred and counted backward toward one. Fiona was usually asleep by the time he reached eighty.

Chapter Sixteen

THE NEXT COUPLE of weeks went by quickly for Fiona. She spent her days with Alabama and Caroline, either together or separately, and her evenings and nights with Hunter. They had more heavy petting nights in his bed, but hadn't gone beyond that. Fiona wanted to, but knew she wasn't ready because every time she thought about doing more than touching, she freaked out and couldn't go through with it. Fiona was beginning to think she'd never be ready, and that killed her. Hunter deserved so much more.

Hunter had begun to encourage her to talk to a professional. He'd told her there was a doctor on base that had experience in dealing with the type of abuse she'd suffered. He'd even given her the doctor's card. He'd spoken with her and she'd agreed to talk to her whenever she was ready. Fiona didn't know if she'd ever be ready, but she carried the woman's card with her wherever she went just in case.

One day when Fiona was hanging out with Alabama, Fiona's cell phone rang. The only calls she ever received were from Hunter's, and now her, friends. It obviously wasn't Alabama calling her, as she was sitting in front of her.

"Hello?"

"Hey, Fee, it's Cookie."

"Hey, Hunter, everything all right?"

"Of course. I'm sorry to have worried you. You with Alabama at her place?"

"Yeah."

"Okay, I'm coming over."

"Are you sure everything's okay?"

"Of course. I'll see you soon?"

"Okay, I'll be waiting."

"Bye."

"Bye."

Fiona looked over to Alabama, only to see her fingers flying on her phone. She was obviously texting someone.

When she was done, Fiona said, "That was Hunter, he said he was coming to pick me up.

"Okay, yeah, okay."

"What's up? Was that Abe?"

Fiona had never been able to remember to call the other men on the team by their real name. If anyone ever listened to them talking they'd think they were crazy since Caroline and Alabama both used the men's real names, and Fiona used their nicknames. It was as if they were talking about completely different people.

"Uh yeah, Christopher is coming home too."

"Do you think they're all right?"

"Yeah, I'm sure it's nothing."

"What? You sound funny, Alabama."

Alabama sighed. "Look, I'm sure Hunter wants to tell you himself, but I'm finding it hard to keep this from you."

"Oh my God, what? You're freaking me out."

"They got called out on a mission. They're leaving tonight."

"*Tonight?*" Fiona couldn't help the shrill tone of her voice. She took a deep breath and tried again. "Tonight? They're leaving tonight?"

"Yeah, and I'm probably going to get my butt kicked for telling you before Hunter could. He's probably nervous as hell about telling you and about leaving you. I know the first time Christopher went on a mission after we got together he was a mess. I'm only telling you this because I think you need to know now and not have it sprung on you."

Fiona nodded, even though she was freaked out, she knew whatever Alabama was about to tell her was serious.

"Christopher made mistakes on that first mission after we got together. He was worried about me and his head wasn't in the right place. When he got back…he…well he hurt me and we almost broke up for good as a result." Seeing the panic on Fiona's face, Alabama hurried on. "We got it worked out, so it's all good. I'm only telling you this so you can do whatever you need to do to convince Hunter you're good and he can keep his head in the game."

Fiona nodded frantically. "I'm sorry you went through whatever it was, and I'm so glad you two worked it out. I don't want Hunter to worry about me. What do I say to him?"

"You'll figure it out. But remember you aren't alone. He might be going on a mission, but you have me and Caroline here. We have your back. Okay?"

"Okay. Thank you for telling me. I probably wouldn't have reacted well if I didn't have a head's up. I appreciate it. Can I call you later?"

"No, don't call. Just get your butt over to Caroline's after Hunter leaves. We'll have a slumber party over there and eat too much and cry over missing our men. Then we'll go shopping tomorrow and spend a crap ton of money. That should hold us over until our men come back to us."

Fiona laughed as Alabama had intended her to.

There was a knock at the door. Alabama went to it, checked the peephole and opened it. Hunter and Abe stood there. Abe immediately reached for Alabama and pulled her into his arms.

"Hey, babe. Hey, Fiona."

"Hey," Fiona answered absently, her eyes on Hunter.

"Hey, Fee. Ready to go?"

"Yeah. See you later, Alabama," Fiona called, as Hunter steered them out the door with his hand on the small of her back.

Fiona didn't say anything as Hunter led them to his car and made sure she was she settled into her seat before walking around to the driver's side. He started it up Fiona fidgeted in her seat, but kept silent. She put her left hand on Hunter's thigh as he drove. She could tell he was tense, and knew Alabama had been right in telling her what was going on. She'd be freaking out right now if she didn't already know. Hell, she'd probably have convinced herself that Hunter was about to break up with her or something.

It was obvious Hunter was dreading telling her he was leaving. Fiona relaxed a little when he put his hand over hers on his lap, liking the skin-on-skin contact and taking comfort from it.

They arrived back at his apartment and they both were silent as they walked up the stairs.

"Let's sit on the balcony, okay?"

"Okay." Fiona kept her voice as soft and soothing as she could.

Cookie sat down on one of the wide patio chairs and pulled Fiona down into his lap. Fiona immediately settled into him and curled one arm around his neck and laid her head against his chest. "Whatever it is, Hunter, it'll be all right." Fiona wanted to settle him as soon as she could. She hated seeing him worked up.

"You know I'm a SEAL." Fiona nodded and Cookie kept speaking. "It's a part of who I am. I don't want to change it. I'm good at what I do. But if you need me to quit, I will."

Fiona sat up at that. "What the hell, Hunter? Why would you even *say* that?"

"We're leaving tonight for a mission, Fee. I have to leave today. This is how it works. Sometimes we get advanced notice, but more often than not, we have to leave as soon as we're notified." Hunter's voice was tortured and he continued. "I can't tell you where we're going or what we're doing. I can't tell you how long we'll be gone. There's a chance I won't come back. There's always a chance I might not come back."

Fiona's eyes filled with tears at his tone of voice. This was what Alabama was talking about. Somehow she had to find the right words to reassure him.

"Hunter, I know you're a SEAL. I thank *God* you're a SEAL every day of my life. Do you think I would've survived getting out of that hell hole if you weren't? I, more than *anyone,* know how important your job is. I'd *never* ask you to quit. I'd kick my own ass if I asked you to quit. Will I worry about you? Of course. Will you worry about me? Of course. But dammit, you can't let either of those things keep you from doing what it is you do best. Am I sad you're leaving? Yes. Am I concerned that I won't know where you are or what you're doing? Hell yeah. But Hunter, I can handle it. You'll come back to me. You *will.* Every time. I believe it and *you* have to believe it. I'm not some little girl that's gonna fall apart every time you leave. Besides, I have Caroline and Alabama to hang out with and go shopping with." She felt Hunter relax a fraction beneath her. Fiona continued, trying to tease Hunter out of his doldrums.

"Besides, you did give me carte blanche to use your credit card, and I plan on using the hell out of it when you're gone." Okay, that was a blatant lie, but Hunter didn't have to know that.

"Only if you buy another sexy nightie for me to see you in when I get back."

Fiona smiled and leaned toward him. "You got it."

"I have to admit, you're taking this much better than I thought you would."

"I know. You stressed yourself out about it too. But Hunter, I have to tell you something…Alabama already told me. She wanted to prepare me."

Cookie frowned. "It wasn't her place."

Fiona could tell Hunter was about to get all worked up, so she interrupted him before he could start. "Yes, it was. You worked yourself into a frenzy. Alabama lived through something with Abe that she didn't want to happen to us. She did us a favor."

Cookie was quiet for a moment digesting what Fiona told him. She was right. Alabama had done the right thing. "You're right. Abe screwed up with Alabama and she was trying to prevent me from doing the same damn thing. But, Fee, frankly, I'm dreading leaving you."

"Since we're being honest, I'm kinda dreading it too, but you need to go, Hunter. I *want* you to go. I'll be okay. I swear."

"Before I leave, I want you to know something," Cookie said in a low voice, running his hand over Fiona's back gently and lovingly.

Fiona curled up into Hunter's chest again. "Okay."

"I love you."

Fiona's head whipped up at Hunter's words and stared at him.

Cookie said it again, "I love you."

"You aren't saying that because you're leaving and you're afraid you're not coming back are you? Because if you are, I'll kick your ass."

Cookie laughed. "No, Fee. I've known I've loved you for a while now, but I was trying to give you time to get used to me and to get used to being mine. I decided now was a good time to let you know. I'm coming back, you can bet the farm on that. I have yet to get inside you."

"Jesus, Hunter, you can't say things like that!"

"I just did."

Fiona smiled at Hunter through her tears. "I…"

Cookie put a finger over her lips. "Don't say it just because I did. Even if it takes you another twenty years to say it, I'll be here. I'm not letting you go just because you haven't said it. Say it when you mean it. When you know deep down in your heart that you mean it. Until then, I'll be here. I'll be annoying you with leaving my socks on the floor and my beard shavings in the sink. I won't let you go. If you leave me, I'll find you. You're mine. Hear me? Mine."

"I hear you."

"Say it." Hunter's words were guttural and desperate.

"Yours."

"Damn straight. Now kiss me."

THAT NIGHT CAROLINE, Fiona, and Alabama sat on Caroline's huge bed. They'd watched Bette Midler in *Beaches* and cried their eyes out. Of course the movie was just an excuse to cry, and they all knew it. None of them wanted to admit they were worried about their men. Belonging to a Navy SEAL wasn't an easy thing. But luckily the women had each other to rely on and to lean on when necessary.

The next morning Caroline was the first to wake up, as usual. She elbowed Fiona and Alabama until they woke up. They took turns getting ready to go out and have some retail therapy.

Around eleven, they were finally ready. Alabama drove them to the mall and they set out, each determined to find something sexy to wear for when their man arrived back home.

They were in the lingerie shop, and Caroline was trying to decide if she should buy a black or red nighty, when something caught Fiona's eye to her right. She turned her head and saw two Hispanic men watching them. A shiver immediately ran down Fiona's spine and she felt lightheaded and sick.

She hated her reaction. The men weren't doing anything wrong. They were watching them because Caroline was loud, probably too loud for the sedate store. The men weren't trying to kidnap them, they weren't even leering at them. But it didn't matter. Just seeing them standing there looking at her, brought her right back to that hell hole in Mexico.

Fiona fell to a crouch in the middle of the store. She put both hands over her head and whimpered.

Caroline heard the sound and looked around in confusion. Seeing Fiona on the ground she immediately dropped the bra she'd been holding, and crouched next to her.

"Fiona? What's wrong? What is it?"

"They're here," Fiona whispered. "We have to get out of here."

"Who's here?" Alabama asked kneeling at her other side.

"Don't let them see you, they'll take you too. We have to hide."

Alabama and Caroline locked eyes over Fiona's shaking body. They weren't exactly sure what was going on, but they had a good idea.

"Fiona, it's safe. They're gone now, come on, get up, we'll go home and have a cup of coffee."

Fiona peeked out from under her arms and saw the two men standing there, looking at them in morbid fascination.

Whispering now, Fiona frantically grabbed her friends' arms. "Okay, they know about me, but you guys can still get out of here. I'll give myself up to them, and you guys go out that other door. Get away. You have to get away. I've already been through it, I can take it. You guys go. Just go."

Caroline saw the look Fiona had shot the two Hispanic men standing nearby. She jerked her chin up at Alabama as she'd seen Matthew do to his team time and time again. Luckily, Alabama had been around them long enough to understand. She let go of Fiona's arm and stood up to ask the men to leave. While she was telling them, she'd tell the other bystanders to leave as well. It was rude to stare.

Fiona saw Alabama start to head toward the men and jerked out of Caroline's hold. "No! Alabama No! Run, dammit, run!" She leaped after Alabama and had enough of a head start over Caroline that she reached Alabama before Caroline could stop her. She grabbed Alabama's arm and jerked her backward. Fiona then rushed up to the now gaping men. "You can't have them, assholes. You can't. Take me back if you have to, but leave them alone!"

The men, obviously surprised at the venom in Fiona's voice, took three quick steps away from her. They looked around in surprise, wondering if the crazy lady was really talking to them.

Caroline had caught Alabama when Fiona had whipped her in her direction, and ran to catch up to Fiona.

"Please, you guys, just go, she's having a flashback. You're making it worse. You didn't do anything wrong, but please, just go," Alabama pleaded with the men as she reached Fiona.

The men, happy to leave the vicinity of the crazy women, fled the store as if they'd suddenly found themselves surrounded by hungry tigers.

Caroline and Alabama each grabbed hold of one of Fiona's arms and held on tightly. She wasn't getting away from them again.

"They're gone, Fiona. They're gone. Come on, sweetie. Sit down."

Fiona collapsed on the floor in the middle of the store in relief. The men had left. They wouldn't take her friends. They wouldn't take *her*. "We have to get out of here in case they come back," she told Caroline and Alabama earnestly. "You don't know them, they won't give up. They'll be back."

"Okay, we'll go," Caroline soothed. She wished with all her heart that the guys were around. Fiona needed Hunter. "Alabama is going to go and get the car. We'll just sit here until she gets back, okay?"

Fiona nodded, closed her eyes and rocked back and forth on the floor, oblivious to the looks she was given by curious shoppers and the concerned looks from her friend.

Caroline sat on the floor of the lingerie shop holding Fiona until Alabama came back. Caroline knew Alabama was hurrying, but it seemed to take way too long for her to arrive back at their sides.

"I've pulled the car around to the back door. The manager said it'd be okay if we took her out that way. I tried to explain some of what's going on. She's worried about her too."

Caroline nodded and took hold of Fiona's head and forced her to look into her own eyes. "Fiona? Alabama has the car here. Can you walk? We're going to go home."

Fiona tried to focus on what Caroline was saying. Why was Caroline there? Was she taken too? "Caroline? Did they get you too?"

Caroline just shook her head sadly. "No, we're safe, sweetie. Come on, let's get out of here, okay?"

Fiona nodded numbly. Getting out of there sounded good to her. The men could come back any second, it was better to leave.

The three friends shuffled out the back door to the waiting car. The manager looked on with sad eyes. Alabama had told her enough of Fiona's suffering for her to feel bad about what had happened in her store.

Caroline and Alabama got Fiona buckled into her seat, and Alabama drove while Caroline sat next to Fiona and held her. Fiona shook uncontrollably all the way home.

After getting Fiona back to Caroline's house, they tucked her into bed and stayed with her until she fell asleep. Neither questioned when Fiona started counting backwards from one thousand. They even joined in when it seemed to calm her more.

Caroline and Alabama sat at the kitchen table,

speechless.

"She needs help. I feel helpless. I don't know what to do," Alabama said sadly.

"All we can do it be there for her."

"Do you think she's gonna remember today?"

"I sure as hell hope not, Alabama. If she does, she's gonna be mortified."

"That's bullcrap. She doesn't have anything to be embarrassed about."

"I know that, and you know that, but I bet anything, she'll be embarrassed anyway."

Alabama then whispered softly, as if afraid she was saying something blasphemous, "I wish the guys were here."

"Me too, Alabama. Me too," Caroline agreed just as quietly.

Chapter Seventeen

FIONA ROLLED OVER with a groan. She felt like crap. The room was dark, but she was starving. Her stomach growling had woken her up. She looked at the clock, at least where the clock should be. It wasn't there. Then Fiona remembered. She was at Caroline's. She and Alabama had spent the night there because the guys had been sent on a mission.

Then Fiona sat bolt upright. Oh no. Jesus. Shopping. The men. Her freak out. Fiona buried her face in her hands. Oh my God. She'd seen those men and thought she was back in Mexico. She'd accused innocent men of horrible things. What if she'd been by herself? What would she have done? She was mortified.

She had to get out of there. Fiona looked around cautiously. She was alone in the room. She could go back home. No. She had no home. She would go back to Hunter's apartment, then go…somewhere. She couldn't stay. Hunter deserved so much better than her. What if she'd freaked out when he was there? She'd be so embarrassed. She was so screwed up in the head.

Fiona tiptoed around the room, finding her shoes and purse and checking to make sure she had everything. She cautiously opened the door to the room. Seeing and hearing no one, she made her way down the hall. When she got to the living room, Fiona saw both Caroline and Alabama sprawled on the sofa sectional. There was an empty bottle of Jack Daniels on the coffee table and several cans of soda lying around as well. They'd obviously gotten hammered as a result of Fiona's actions the previous day.

Tears sprang to Fiona's eyes. Jesus, they'd been so embarrassed over what she'd done they had to get drunk to make it through the night. As Fiona headed toward the door she knew she'd never forget the sight of her first and only true friends, passed out on the couch because of something she'd done.

CAROLINE WOKE UP and groaned. Jesus, she'd had way too much to drink. She knew better, but she'd been so worried about Fiona, she'd just kept drinking. She saw Alabama still passed out next to her, and nudged her with her foot.

"Hey, Alabama, get up. Let's go check on Fiona."

Alabama groaned, but sat up gingerly. "Why'd you let me drink so much last night?"

"Me? You were the one encouraging *me* to keep going."

"Okay, so we might have been encouraging each other."

They smiled at each other. "Come on, let's go get Fiona and get the awkward crap out of the way first, then we can make a huge breakfast, choke it down, and figure out what we're gonna do and how to help her."

Alabama led the way toward the room where they'd left Fiona last night. They stood there in shock when they pushed the door open and saw the empty bed. Caroline turned and left the room as if she wasn't feeling sick a moment ago.

"Come on, Alabama, we have to get over to Hunter's. She probably woke up early and thought she'd be polite and not wake us. She was probably also embarrassed and wanted to avoid us. We have to go get her and let her know she has nothing to be embarrassed about."

The two women threw on clean clothes and raced out of the house without a thought to their appearance. Their only focus was finding their friend and reassuring her.

Once they'd arrived at Hunter's apartment, Alabama and Caroline knocked on the door, when there was no answer, they proceeded to *beat* on the door, calling Fiona's name over and over.

When she still didn't answer they could only conclude that Fiona wasn't there. "The car!" Alabama raced back to the parking lot. Neither Carline or Alabama had been concerned about looking for Hunter's car when they'd first arrived.

Seeing Hunter's parking space empty, Alabama whispered, "Shit." Her legs folded under her and she was sitting on the ground.

Caroline slumped to the ground next to her friend, stymied about what they should do next.

For the second time in as many days, Alabama said, "I wish the guys were here."

Caroline could only nod in agreement.

FIONA DROVE FOR a long as she could. She was tired, but wanted to get as far north as possible. She shook her head. North meant away from Mexico, that was the only thing running through her head at the moment. Fiona had to protect her friends, and the best way to do that, was to get away from them.

She made it as far as the outskirts of San Francisco before she had to pull off the road. Fiona debated sleeping in the car, but then figured that would make it even easier for the kidnappers to overpower her. Then she considered stopping at a flea-bag motel that rented by the hour, but again realized if the kidnappers came for her there, most likely no one would come to her aid because they were all trying to stay under the radar.

Fiona ended up pulling into a high-end hotel. She knew she wasn't exactly dressed to blend in, her sweats and too-big T-shirt definitely made her stand out, but in the end, decided everyone would be too disciplined to say anything to her about it.

She checked in, using Hunter's credit card, and went up to her room. Fiona had no luggage, but at the moment she didn't care. She lay back on the bed and closed her eyes. She was terrified and exhausted.

Fiona tried to reason out what was going on. She remembered getting back to Hunter's apartment and seeing the Hispanic men from the mall in the parking lot…at least she thought it was the same men. She had to run, had to get out of there. She hadn't even gone up to the apartment, just raced out of the parking lot and headed north.

Fiona shut her eyes. She'd just take a short nap then get up and get going again. She fell back on what had always worked before when she was stressed out, she counted. One thousand. Nine hundred ninety nine. Nine hundred ninety eight…

Six hours later, Fiona woke up disoriented and confused. Where was she? This didn't look like Caroline's house. She sat up. It was most definitely a hotel room, but she had no recollection of checking in. Snippets of the day before slowly started filtering into her brain.

I'm losing it. Jesus, I'm losing it. Is this really happening or am I dreaming it? Did my kidnappers really find me? Fiona couldn't figure out what was real and what wasn't. She wanted Hunter, but he was…somewhere. He was off saving someone else and she had no way of getting in touch with him.

As she fell deeper into the delusion that she was being hunted, Fiona thought about Hunter… *He found me in the middle of the Mexican jungle and he wasn't even looking. He'll find me here. I just have to stay one step ahead of the kidnappers and wait for Hunter.*

"WE HAVE TO do something, Caroline," Alabama implored her friend. "We can't just sit here and wait for her to come home. It's obvious she isn't going to just come back and say, 'Hey, sorry I worried you, I'm back.'"

"Something's really wrong, Alabama," Caroline stated the obvious. "Fiona really thought those men were there to take her back to Mexico. What if she still thinks that? Is that even possible?"

"I have no idea, but, Jesus, Caroline. If that's what she thinks, there's no telling where she is. We have to call the commander. He can get in touch with Hunter. He has to know."

"But what if they can't come home right now? That would just freak Hunter out and put him and the rest of the team in danger."

"I know, but what if it was us in trouble? You know Christopher or Matthew would never forgive us if they weren't notified."

"Okay, I'll call Commander Hurt and let him know what's going on."

Caroline called the base and left a message for the team commander to call her back as soon as he could. She tried to make sure the Petty Officer who took the message understood it was literally a life and death situation and that the commander needed to call her as he got back into his office.

Alabama sat up suddenly. "Oh my God, why didn't we think of this before? What about Tex?"

"Tex! Shit! Yes, you're a genius, Alabama!"

Caroline scrambled for her phone. If anyone could find Fiona, it'd be Tex. She scrolled through her contacts and clicked on his name.

"What's wrong?" Leave it to Tex to cut right to the chase.

"Fiona's missing and Hunter and the others are on a mission."

"Talk to me."

"We were shopping yesterday and there were two Hispanic men minding their own business in the same store we were in. Fiona saw them and literally freaked. She had a flashback or something and we had to get out of mall through the back door of the store. We brought her home, but when we woke up, she was gone. She's not at Hunter's apartment and his car is missing. We think she's stuck in the flashback or something. We don't know what to do."

"Have you contacted the commander?"

"Yeah, I just got off the phone with someone on the base and left a message for him to call us back. Alabama thought about you. You can find her can't you, Tex?"

"Yeah, I'll find her. Keep trying to get through to the commander, I'll see what I can do from this end."

"Thank you, Tex. Oh, and she's got Hunter's credit card. Hunter gave it to her to use, she didn't steal it."

Tex's voice lost its edge a bit. "I wouldn't have thought she did, Ice. That's good she has it. I'll find her and get back to you as soon as I can."

"Okay. Thank you so much. We didn't know what to do."

"You did the right thing in calling me. Later, Ice."

"Bye, Tex."

Caroline turned to Alabama and told her unnecessarily, "Tex said he'd find her."

Alabama nodded. "Okay, if he said he'd find her, he will. We just have to pray it's soon."

THE PHONE ON the nightstand rang and Fiona nearly jumped a foot. She stared at it. Was it Hunter? Was it the kidnappers? Had they found her? She struggled for a moment between wanting to answer the phone and wanting to run out of the room and jump in the car and keep driving. Fiona dug down deep to the courage she'd been missing for the last day or so, and reached for the phone.

"Hello?"

"Fiona, it's Cookie's friend, Tex. Don't hang up."

Fiona sagged in relief. She remembered Hunter talking about Tex. Thank God he'd found her. "Tex?" she whispered, "I'm so scared. They found me."

On the other end of the line, Tex sagged in his seat. Thank fuck she knew who he was, but Jesus, he had to do everything right here, and he wasn't sure what that was. Fiona was obviously stuck in the delusion she was being hunted, and all it would take would be one wrong word out of his mouth and she'd run again. Tex decided it'd be better to cater to her delusion for the moment instead of trying to convince her she was imagining everything.

"Fiona, listen to me. Cookie told you about what I can do with computers right? Well, I've got them covered. I know where the kidnappers are, and they're still back in Riverton. They don't realize you've left yet. You're safe right there where you are. Just stay put.

Order room service, ask them to leave it outside your door and put everything on the credit card. I've got your credit card secured, so no one else will be able to trace it. Do you hear me? You're safe right where you are."

Tex didn't want Fiona opening the door to possibly a Hispanic hotel worker, or anyone, and freaking out again. He knew she was safe in the hotel for the moment. He'd tracked her down with one short search of Cookie's credit card. Fiona wasn't really trying to hide, she was just running scared.

"Okay Tex. I'll wait to hear from you. Am I really safe here? They don't know I left?" Her voice was low and trembled with emotion.

"No, sweetheart. They have no idea where you are." Tex was being completely honest.

"Is Hunter coming to find me again?"

Tex's heart almost broke. "I'm working on it, Fee. You know he's on a mission right?"

"Yeah, I know. That's why they came now, they knew he was gone and wasn't here to protect me."

"We're trying to get Cookie home so he can come and get you. Remember what I said, don't move. Stay hunkered down there."

"Okay, Tex. I will."

"I'm going to call you every four hours, Fiona. You be there to answer the phone. Okay? Every four hours."

"I got it. I'll be here."

"Good. Drink lots of water and make sure you order food from the hotel. Keep up your strength." Tex figured if he ordered Fiona to do things, she'd be more likely to follow through.

"Yeah, okay." She paused, and said in a child-like voice, "I want Hunter."

"He'll be there as soon as he can, Fiona. Hang on for him, baby."

Tex was reluctant to hang up, but he had some other calls to make. He had to get Cookie home. His woman needed him. Now.

"Okay, I'll wait for Hunter."

"I'll talk to you in four hours, Fiona. Four hours. No more, no less. Make sure you answer the phone."

"Okay, Tex. Bye."

Tex hung up the phone and swore long and loud. He knew Cookie hadn't expected this to happen. Fiona obviously needed help dealing with what had happened to her. His first call was to the commander. He had to get Cookie home. His woman needed him.

COOKIE SLAMMED OPEN the door to Caroline and Wolf's house. They'd been knee deep in a "situation" in a not-so-well-known country in Africa, when Wolf had pulled him aside and told him about Fiona. It'd taken both Benny and Abe holding him back so he wouldn't go running off half-cocked and getting both himself and his team killed. The team had talked it over and decided, with the blessing of their commander, to pull back and allow another SEAL team to take over.

They all knew how unusual it was for them to be even be *given* the chance to pull back. Usually when it came to Uncle Sam, there *was* no option. The mission came first, always. But apparently Tex had personally discussed the situation with the commander and convinced him for the need of an immediate withdrawal of Cookie and the rest of the team.

All six men had immediately agreed to get the hell out of Africa, and get back to California so Cookie could help his woman.

Wolf was right behind Cookie when he entered his house. Caroline and Alabama were there and Caroline immediately ran into Matthew's arms.

"I'm sorry, I'm so sorry, Hunter. I should have kept a better eye on her."

"Tell me what happened from the beginning, Ice." Cookie's voice was hard and even, as if he was holding on to his temper and sanity by his fingernails.

"Careful, Cookie," Wolf warned, not liking the tone he was taking with Caroline.

"It's okay, Matthew," Caroline reassured him. Turning back to Hunter she told him what had happened at the store and what they'd done afterwards.

"It sounds like you did everything right, Ice. You got her out of the store and you and Alabama stayed with her."

"But we got drunk and she snuck out."

"I know, but remember she got away from me too when we were in Texas. She's an adult, you couldn't have watched over her all day and all night. Even if you weren't drunk, she still could've left while you were sleeping. Desperate people can manage to do things that people who are in their right mind never can."

"She took your car, and Tex traced her to San Francisco. She's in a hotel up there."

"Yeah, he debriefed me as soon as we landed. I'm headed to the airport to get her, I just have to make one stop first."

"You're stopping somewhere?" Alabama questioned harshly.

Cookie turned to her and defended his actions, even though he didn't really feel he had to. "Yeah, I'm collecting Dr. Hancock. I wanted Fiona to see her and talk to her about everything she went through in Mexico, but she obviously never followed through. I'm not giving Fee a choice now. I don't know how to help her, but I know Dr. Hancock can. So I'm picking her up, I've already contacted her and she agreed, and we're going to fly up there and bring Fiona home."

"Sorry, Hunter. Jesus, I've been so worried about

her. I know you'd never take her safety for granted. Go. Bring her home." Alabama sounded so contrite, Hunter couldn't help but take the two steps to her side and bring her into him for a quick hug.

"She'll be home as soon as I can get her here. I'm taking Benny with us, but Dr. Hancock thinks it would be best if Fiona didn't see him at all. He'll drive my car back down here while we go up to the hotel room to get Fiona. We'll fly back as soon as Dr. Hancock says it's okay. Abe will be over here to the house as soon as he can. He and the others had to debrief with the commander."

Cookie let go of Alabama and held her at arm's length with his hands on her shoulders. He watched as she nodded and he squeezed her shoulders reassuringly.

"Okay, go get her, Hunter. Bring Fiona home"

Caroline, Wolf, and Alabama watched as Cookie strode out of the house, back to the car at the curb. Benny was behind the wheel. They were on one of the most important missions of their lives, and everyone knew it.

Chapter Eighteen

FIONA ANSWERED THE phone after it rang only once. "Tex?"

"Yeah, babe, it's me. How're you holding up?" Tex had kept his promise and called Fiona every four hours for the last three days. It had taken that long for him to get a hold of the commander, to convince him it was a life or death situation, for Wolf's SEAL team to get back to the States, and for Cookie to get his ass on a plane headed up to San Francisco.

Fiona had answered the phone every time Tex had called. They were both exhausted, but she hadn't missed one call.

"You eat yet?"

"Yeah, I ordered an omelet this morning."

"Okay, that's good. Today's the day, Fiona."

Fiona sucked in a breath. She'd been so confused over the last few days and Tex had been her lifeline. She vacillated between knowing she was losing her mind because she knew no one was after her, to being convinced the kidnappers were waiting downstairs in the lobby to snatch her if she left the room. Tex had called, just as he said he would, every few hours and helped calm her down.

"I'm losing my mind, Tex. I want to go home…back to Hunter's apartment. No one's after me are they?" The last was said in a sad whisper.

"Fiona, Cookie will be there in a couple of hours. Sit tight. He'll be there, and you'll be just fine. Don't leave now, not right before he gets to you." When Tex didn't hear any response, he continued. "I'll call you when he's standing outside your door, so you know it's him and you can let him in. Do you understand?"

"Yes." Fiona's voice was small and wobbly.

"Okay, I'll call back in a couple of hours. Stay in the room; take a nap if you need to. Cookie's coming for you, Fee. I'll talk to you soon."

Tex hung up the phone and paced the room. His prosthetic leg, for once, wasn't hurting. He could only think about Fiona and about her state of mind. She'd been through hell, and he'd been right there with her for the last three days. Tex never knew what her state of mind would be when he'd call. Sometimes Fiona seemed mostly lucid, like this last call, other times she was completely freaked out, convinced the kidnappers were right outside her door.

It was those times that had taken every bit of psychological training he'd ever had. He'd convinced her to do things like go into the bathroom and crouch down in the bathtub until they were "gone." He'd lied and told her he'd tapped into the hotel cameras and had seen the men leave the hallway, even though no one had ever been there in the first place.

He'd talked Cookie into bringing the doctor with him when he went to Fiona. She needed the help, more than anyone he'd ever met. Well, he'd never *met* Fiona, but he'd spoken to her enough over the last seventy hours, that he felt like he knew her.

Tex couldn't wait to hear from Cookie that he'd landed. It was time to end this.

COOKIE CLICKED OFF the phone with Tex and waited for Fee to open the door. Tex had said he'd call Fiona and let her know he was there and that it was safe to open the hotel door. Cookie had said good-bye to Benny in the parking lot after they'd arrived in a taxi from the airport. Benny understood why he couldn't see Fiona right now, and even if he didn't like it, he knew it was for the best. He'd wrung a promise out of Cookie to be able to come over and see Fiona as soon as Cookie thought she was well enough when they got home.

It wasn't even a minute after hanging up with Tex that Cookie saw the hotel door open an inch, then suddenly Fiona was in his arms. She'd opened the door and thrown herself at him after verifying it really was him at her door.

Cookie could literally feel every muscle in his body relax. He'd been so stressed for the last three days and it was all he could do not to dissolve into a hysterical fit of tears. One hand went around Fiona's waist and the other curled around the back of her head and he held her to him as he backed her into the room and toward the bed.

Fiona could barely say a word. Hunter was here. He was *here*.

"You came."

"I came. I'll *always* come for you." Cookie said the words as if they were the most important words he'd ever said and *would* ever say in his life.

They sat on the bed and after Fiona straddled his lap, Cookie rocked Fiona back and forth. They both needed the contact with each other. They'd each been through their own type of hell.

Finally Cookie loosened his hold, just enough to pull away to look into Fiona's face.

"Fiona?"

"Yeah?"

"Can you tell me what's going on?" Cookie had to see where her head was at. Was she still in the midst of the delusion that she was running from her kidnappers, or was she lucid enough to know she'd imagined the entire thing?

"I…I'm not sure. I think I screwed up."

Cookie shook his head and brought his hands up to Fiona's face and held her face still while he spoke to her. His thumbs caressed the underside of her jaw and he spoke earnestly to her.

"You didn't screw up, Fee. *I* did. I should've made sure I took care of you before I left. I was afraid something like this would happen. But I learned my lesson. I'm not going anywhere until I fix this. Okay?"

Fiona felt the tears start, but couldn't stop them. "I'm sorry. I didn't mean to cause so many problems. I just…they…I can't figure it all out in my head."

"Shhhh, we'll figure it out together. For now, I want you to meet someone. She's with me. Don't be afraid." Cookie gestured toward the door and a short, but kindhearted looking, woman walked in the room. She was wearing a pair of jeans and looked to be about five months pregnant. She waddled a bit as she walked, but the look on her face was open and friendly.

"This is Dr. Hancock. She came with me to help you deal with what's happening. She's with me."

Fiona looked from the woman, who'd stopped right inside the door, back to Hunter. In a low whispered voice Fiona said sadly, "They weren't ever after me were they? I dreamed it all up didn't I? That's why you brought a shrink with you. I'm going crazy."

Cookie touched his forehead to Fiona's and tried to think what he should say. Luckily, the doctor answered for him.

"Fiona, the mind is a powerful thing. I'm sure you've seen videos of people wearing those virtual reality goggles, right? They know they aren't on a roller coaster, but with those goggles on they can't stop their body was swaying and rolling as if they really *were* on a roller coaster. You've had an experience much like that. Deep down you knew those men you saw weren't after you, but based on what happened to you, your conscious mind did what it had to do to protect itself. You're not going crazy. You're perfectly normal. If you hadn't reacted as you had, I would've been even more worried about you."

Fiona looked up at Hunter again. "I'm sorry. I'm so sorry. You were on a mission…"

"Stop. You're more important than any mission. I told you that before and I'll keep saying it until you believe it. I'd scale mountains for you. I'd quit today if you needed me. You. Come. First. Period. No more "sorry's." Let's get home. Talk to Dr. Hancock. We'll figure it out. Together."

Fiona wrapped her arms around Hunter and sighed when she felt his arms surround her again. She nodded.

Cookie stood up with Fee in his arms. He'd swung

her around so one arm was around her back and the other was under her knees. "Close your eyes, Fee. I'll get us out of here. You just relax. Trust me."

"I do, Hunter. I knew you'd come for me and I'd be safe." She gripped Hunter tightly and buried her head in his neck, closing her eyes as Hunter had asked.

"You're safe, Fee. Safe with me. Always."

COOKIE CARRIED FIONA into his apartment while Dr. Hancock followed close behind. She'd talked to Fiona off and on while they'd flown back to southern California. The doctor wanted to get an idea of where Fiona's head was at and the best way to go about getting her the help she needed.

Cookie wanted to cry when he'd heard Fiona tell Dr. Hancock that she'd tried to be brave for *him*. He hadn't wanted Fiona to suppress her feelings, but he *had* told her over and over how impressed he was with her bravery and courage.

He carried her into their room and put Fiona softly on the bed. She didn't stir. She'd been exhausted from trying to hide from imaginary kidnappers as well as answering the phone every four hours when Tex had called. Cookie knew he owed Tex everything. Anything the man ever needed, was his. He'd kept his woman safe. There was no way to repay that. Cookie wouldn't forget it. Ever. He kissed Fiona on the forehead and smoothed her hair back from her head gently. God, she'd scared the shit out of him.

Cookie left the room and went back to where Dr. Hancock was waiting for him.

"What do you think? Do I need to bring her in to the hospital for in-patient treatment?" It wasn't what Cookie wanted to do, but he would if the doctor thought it was what Fiona needed.

"I don't think so. She seems more lucid with you around. You can't leave her alone though, Hunter. If you need to go to work or if you're called away, you'll need to admit her for her own good.

"I'm not going anywhere. It's already been cleared by the commander. If we get called out, the others will cover it. He knows Fiona comes first."

"Okay, good. She'll need daily sessions at first. Then, depending on how those go, we can slowly taper them off. The good news is that I think she *wants* to get better."

"Of course she does," Cookie said heatedly.

"There is no 'of course' about it, Hunter," Dr. Hancock said sadly. "You'd be surprised how many women can't move past what happened to them, what was done to them. They can't get past the abuse and they spiral down into a life of drugs and sometimes prostitution. Even though they were sexually abused, they aren't able to acclimate back into society." Waiting to make sure Hunter understood her words, the doctor nodded, then continued. "Okay, stay with her tonight and bring her in to see me in the morning. I'll probably start out meeting with her alone, then I'll see if she'll allow you to come in as well. Since you were there and a big part of her rescue, I think it'll help."

"I can't thank you enough, Doctor. I should've called you long before now."

"Yes, you should have. But what's done is done. Fiona is getting help now. And if it's any consolation, I think she's going to be fine. You were right. She *is* tough. She *is* brave. That'll get her through this."

Cookie saw the doctor out and watched as she got into an SUV sitting in the parking lot. Her husband had obviously been waiting for her. Cookie stood there, as the car disappeared into the night, thinking he'd been lucky. More than lucky. Cookie turned around and headed back inside, to Fiona.

Chapter Nineteen

FIONA SMILED AT Caroline and Alabama. A week after her "freak out," as Fiona was calling it, she felt a lot better about everything that had happened. At first she'd refused to talk to either of the women, thinking they hated her. But after several meetings with Dr. Hancock, she'd finally reached out to her friends.

Thank God for true friends. Hunter had brought her over to Caroline's house and he, Wolf, and Abe had watched some sports game on television while the three women worked everything out between them in the basement.

Hunter had refused to leave her side over the last week and Fiona was inwardly glad. She'd told him several times that he didn't have to babysit her, but he'd countered, telling her he wasn't babysitting, but supporting and lending an ear when she needed it.

Fiona had only taken one step inside Wolf's house before she'd been engulfed in both Caroline's and Alabama's arms. They'd cried and laughed and that was before they'd even talked.

They'd spent hours in the basement talking through what had happened and both laughing and crying about it. When Fiona tried to apologize, Caroline lost her mind and ranted for a full ten minutes about kidnappers and nosy shoppers and sex slave rings, and Fiona hadn't had the heart to try to apologize again.

It was eleven at night when Wolf finally cracked open the basement door and hollered, "Is it safe to come down?"

Laughing, the women had answered yes.

All three men came down the stairs and went right to their women.

Cookie scooped Fiona up and plopped her into his lap as he sat on the floor by the couch. He leaned back against it and Fiona snuggled down into his arms as she usually did.

Wolf sat next to Caroline on the sofa and pulled her into him so that she was resting her head on his chest.

Abe went to the big easy chair and sat down, motioning for Alabama to come to him. She went over to him and straddled him, putting her knees on either side of his lap and folding in on him like a boneless rag doll.

"We were worried about you, Fiona," Wolf said, rubbing his hand up and down Caroline's back.

"I know, and I'm sorry."

"No, don't be sorry. It's what friends do. You do

know you've got some pretty serious friends here, right?"

"I do. And you'll never know how much I appreciate it. I've never had true friends before, only acquaintances." Fiona loved the feel of Hunter's arms around her. It made talking about scary stuff somehow easier.

"I've already apologized to Caroline and Alabama, but I'm sorry you guys had to come back from your mission to get me. I honestly didn't mean for that to happen. What you guys do is important. I can't imagine if you got called away from *my* rescue."

Without raising his voice, Abe answered calmly. "You would've been rescued, Fiona. We don't operate independently. If we got called off of your rescue, another group would've been called in and you still would've been saved. Every SEAL team covers for each other."

"But…"

"No buts, Fiona. And just so you know, you're ours now. You're mine. You're Wolf's, you're Benny's…you're all of ours. If you're in trouble, we're there."

Cookie held Fiona tighter as she sobbed in his arms. He let her cry. She needed to hear Abe's words. Really hear them.

"So if you're in trouble, it's like our own women are

in trouble. If you call me, I'll come running. If Alabama calls Cookie, he'll go to her. So you see, Cookie is your man, but he's actually a package deal."

Fiona looked up finally. Her face was blotchy and red from crying, but she tried to smile at Abe. She hiccupped once, then got herself together.

"I've been talking to Dr. Hancock a lot this week, as you all know. I've tried to come to terms with what happened to me, what happens to women all over the world every single day. But the one thing I couldn't do was see any good that came out of what happened to me. Yes, I met Hunter and I'll forever thank God for that, but I was having a hard time coming up with anything else for my list. Until now. Until you guys. I never dreamed I'd find a man of my own, nevertheless a family full of brothers and sisters."

"You might not like it once we all get up in your business, Fiona," Wolf warned her seriously.

Fiona chuckled. "You're right, but once I can think about it, I'll remember how lonely I was and how much better my life is now that you're in it, and I'll thank my lucky stars you all came into my life."

A comfortable silence fell over the group.

Cookie broke it with a chuckle. "If you're both done wooing my woman, I think we'll be going home now."

Everyone laughed and Fiona smacked Hunter on the arm.

Wolf stood up and pulled Caroline up with him. "It's time we headed to bed ourselves. Abe, you guys staying here?"

Abe looked at Alabama with raised eyebrows. Since Alabama had lived here in the basement for a bit while Abe was getting his act together, they knew they were welcome and frequently took Wolf and Caroline up on the offer to stay the night instead of driving home.

"Yeah, we can stay here." Alabama's words were slurred. She was already half asleep.

Cookie stood up with Fiona in his arms. He carried her up the stairs and out the door without giving her a chance to say good-bye. He knew she'd see her friends again, most likely the next day. The trip home was done in silence. Cookie hoped the night had been a turning point in her recovery.

When they arrived home, Cookie turned to Fiona and ordered, "Stay," as she reached for the door handle. She smiled at him and did as she was told.

Cookie came around the side of the car and opened her door and lifted Fiona out.

"You know I can walk. You don't have to cart me around everywhere."

"You weigh less than the pack I carry on missions. Now hush."

Fiona only smiled and snuggled deeper into her man.

Cookie carried Fiona up the stairs into their room. For what was quickly becoming a habit for them, he laid her down gently on the bed and took off her shoes. Looking into her eyes, Cookie unfastened her pants and eased them down her legs.

Fiona lay on Hunter's bed and watched as he carefully undressed her. She didn't feel even a second of unease. This was Hunter. He wouldn't do anything to hurt her. Ever.

Fiona watched as Hunter took his shirt off and threw it toward the hamper in the corner of the room. He then sat on the bed and leaned over and took off his boots. Next came his pants and boxers. Only when he was completely naked did he lean over Fiona and lift the shirt off her head. Fiona dutifully raised her arms to allow him to remove her shirt. Once that was done, he reached under her back and unhooked her bra. His actions were clinical rather than romantic, but he still made her feel cherished.

Over the last week, Fiona slowly came to terms with what had happened. As part of her therapy, Dr. Hancock had suggested she go back to the mall and the place where she'd had her "episode." She hadn't wanted to do it, but Hunter had encouraged her and promised he wouldn't leave her side.

They'd gone and walked around the mall for hours. Slowly, Fiona lost her nervousness and enjoyed the day with Hunter. Even when a group of Hispanic men walked by, she hadn't freaked out, but of course having Hunter right there with her probably had a lot to do with it.

After they'd walked by the men, Hunter had steered her into a nearby hallway and kissed the hell out of her. He'd claimed it was a reward for "good behavior." Fiona had only laughed and kissed him again.

Hunter hadn't ever made her feel guilty or bad for what had happened. Dr. Hancock had invited Hunter into their sessions and Fiona had to admit, at first she wasn't happy. She hadn't ever wanted Hunter to learn what the kidnappers had done to her, but after a few sessions she had to admit it was a good call on the doctor's part.

Hunter had to hear what had happened and she'd had to tell him. It'd solidified their relationship in a way that they didn't have before.

Cookie had guessed what Fiona had been through, but hearing it from her, hearing how she felt and how she'd endured, made Cookie realize how lucky he was that Fiona was here with him. There were so many things that could've gone differently...from the men selling her, to their hurting her, to them overdosing her by accident, to her being rescued, their trek through the jungle, the firefight as they waited for the helicopter, the flying bullets, the withdrawal...Cookie knew he could go on and on. But the bottom line was that they were here. Now. Together. Cookie knew they were meant to be together, otherwise any of those things could have ended differently.

As Fiona lay in bed next to Hunter, she knew there was no place she'd rather be.

"I love you, Hunter."

Without hesitation Cookie responded, not making a big deal out of hearing the words from Fiona's lips for the first time. "I love you too, Fee. You're my everything."

Tonight wasn't the night they'd make love, but Fiona knew it'd be soon. Hunter hadn't ever pushed her for it, and she knew he wouldn't. Fiona had talked to Dr. Hancock about sex and how she felt, and while Dr. Hancock cautioned Fiona to go slowly, she'd also encouraged her to do what felt right, when it felt right. Fiona knew she would have to be the one to make the first move, and she would. For now, she and Hunter were enjoying each other's company.

Fiona snuggled deeper into Hunter's embrace. He was always so warm, just one more thing in a long list of things that Fiona loved about him. The feel of his naked body against her own was comforting, instead of horrifying.

"Stop thinking, Fee. Go to sleep."

Fiona smiled. She loved this man more than she

thought possible. As she drifted off to sleep, she smiled she heard Hunter murmur, "Mine, I'll never leave you. You'll never have another night of fear in your life."

Epilogue

FIONA LAY ON Hunter's chest panting and trying to recover. Jesus, he was going to kill her. That was the third orgasm he'd given her that night, and she'd never felt better or more loved.

"I think you've killed me," Fiona mock complained, while Hunter tried to catch his breath as he lay under her satiated body.

Fiona watched as a satisfied smile broke out on Hunter's face. She licked his nipple once more and grinned even wider at the shudder that made its way through his body. She felt him jerk inside her.

"I love you, Mr. Knox."

"I love you, Mrs. Knox."

They'd flown to Vegas and gotten married without telling anyone. Their friends hadn't talked to them for at least two days in protest, but Fiona wouldn't have changed anything about their wedding. She hadn't wanted to make a big deal out of their marriage. For her, it was a natural continuation of their love. She'd had enough of being in the spotlight, Fiona had just wanted to marry Hunter and continue on with their lives.

Hunter had protested at first. He'd wanted to give her a huge wedding and invite all their friends, and their friends, and *their* friends. It wasn't until Fiona explained *why* she wanted a small wedding with just the two of them, that he'd relented.

Now, anytime anyone tried to complain about missing their wedding, Hunter would take them aside and bluntly explain it wasn't any of their business why they'd done what they had, and warned them not to bring it up again.

"I hate to bring up anything other than how much of a man-stud you are since we're lying still attached in our bed, but I'm worried about Mozart," Fiona said drowsily.

"I know, me too."

"Why is he so obsessed with that guy?"

"I'm not completely sure, but I think it has to do with his sister. I know she was killed when she was little and they never found the guy who did it. I think that's why Mozart joined the SEALs in the first place, so he could eventually track down the guy, since the cops had essentially closed the case."

"Do you think he'll ever find him?"

"I have no idea, but I know he sure is trying his

damnedest."

"Do you think the guy he's hunting up near Big Bear is the killer?"

"I don't know, but I'd say so. Mozart doesn't make many mistakes, not when it comes to something as important as this."

Fiona nodded. "I feel bad."

"Me too. But before you ask, I'm not going to sit him down for a chat about it," Cookie told Fiona resolutely.

Fiona giggled, imaging Hunter and Mozart "chatting" about their feelings. Her giggle turned into a moan when she felt Hunter grow harder inside of her. She wiggled, urging him to do something."

"Again, Fee?"

"Oh yeah, again."

"You know, maybe you need to go and see Dr. Hancock about this insatiable need you have," Hunter teased.

"If I have a problem, so do you." Fiona sat up in Hunter's lap and swiveled her hips, loving the feel of his hard length inside her. She put her hands on his chest and leaned into him.

"You're right, I do. So let's see if we can't do something about it."

Cookie smiled up at his woman. Fiona had come so

far since the night he'd found her shaking and scared out of her mind in the hotel room in San Francisco. He'd never forget the anxiety he'd felt as he tried to get to her from his mission in Africa. She hadn't had many relapses since then, and nothing like that time.

The first time Fiona had initiated sex when they'd gotten back from San Francisco, Cookie had tried to resist, not believing she'd had enough time to process everything that had happened to her. She'd insisted she was fine and it wasn't until Cookie had wrung a promise out of her to stop if she felt even an inkling of unease, that he'd continued. That first time was special.

Cookie had been with his fair share of women, but nothing in his entire life, compared to the first time he'd eased into Fiona's warm, welcome, wet body. She hadn't even flinched, just held on to his face and looked him in the eyes as he'd entered her. She'd responded to his, "You okay with this, Fee?" with words he'd memorized. She'd said, "I'm perfect, Hunter. When you hold me in your arms, I can't think of anything but you." Even with her relapse, Fiona was still the strongest person Cookie had ever met.

He rolled over so Fiona was under him. He brushed her hair out of her face and smoothed it behind her ear.

"Mine."

"Yours," Fiona immediately returned with a smile.

Blocking everything and everyone out of his mind except for pleasuring his wife, Cookie bent down toward Fiona. He couldn't ask for anything else in this world. He had it all right here in his arms.

Look for the next book in the
SEAL of Protection Series:
Marrying Caroline.

Discover other titles by Susan Stoker

SEAL of Protection Series

Protecting Caroline

Protecting Alabama

Protecting Fiona

Marrying Caroline (novella)

Protecting Summer

Protecting Cheyenne

Protecting Jessyka

Protecting Julie (novella)

Protecting Melody

Protecting the Future

Delta Force Heroes Series

Rescuing Rayne

Assisting Aimee (loosely related to DF)

Rescuing Emily

Rescuing Harley

Rescuing Kassie (TBA)

Rescuing Casey (TBA)

Rescuing Wendy (TBA)

Rescuing Mary (TBA)

Badge of Honor: Texas Heroes Series

Justice for Mackenzie
Justice for Mickie
Justice for Corrie
Justice for Laine (novella)
Shelter for Elizabeth
Justice for Boone
Shelter for Adeline (TBA)
Justice for Sidney (TBA)
Shelter for Blythe (TBA)
Justice for Milena (TBA)
Shelter for Sophie (TBA)
Justice for Kinley (TBA)
Shelter for Promise (TBA)
Shelter for Koren (TBA)
Shelter for Penelope (TBA)

Beyond Reality Series

Outback Hearts
Flaming Hearts
Frozen Hearts

Writing as Annie George

Stepbrother Virgin (erotic novella)

Connect with Susan Online

Susan's Facebook Profile and Page:
www.facebook.com/authorsstoker
www.facebook.com/authorsusanstoker

Follow Susan on Twitter:
www.twitter.com/Susan_Stoker

Find Susan's Books on Goodreads:
www.goodreads.com/SusanStoker

Email: Susan@StokerAces.com

Website: www.StokerAces.com

To sign up for Susan's Newsletter go to:
http://bit.ly/SusanStokerNewsletter

Or text: STOKER to 24587 for text alerts on your mobile device

About the Author

New York Times, *USA Today,* and *Wall Street Journal* Bestselling Author Susan Stoker has a heart as big as the state of Texas, where she lives, but this all-American girl has also spent the last fourteen years living in Missouri, California, Colorado, and Indiana. She's married to a retired Army man who now gets to follow *her* around the country.

She debuted her first series in 2014 and quickly followed that up with the SEAL of Protection Series, which solidified her love of writing and creating stories readers can get lost in.

If you enjoyed this book, or any book, please consider leaving a review. It's appreciated by authors more than you'll know.